Nothing to Say

Gerard Mannix Flynn has worked in the arts for almost thirty years. As well as writing the play *James X*, he has also worked extensively in the performing arts both on stage and in film. He is a member of Aosdána. *Nothing to Say* was translated into German and published by Sachon in 1989.

GERARD MANNIX FLYNN

Nothing to Say

THE LILLIPUT PRESS
DUBLIN

First published 1983 by
WARD RIVER PRESS LTD
Knocksedan House,
Swords, Co. Dublin, Ireland

Revised edition published 2003 by
THE LILLIPUT PRESS LTD
62–63 Sitric Road, Arbour Hill,
Dublin 7, Ireland
www.lilliputpress.ie

A CIP record for this title is available
from The British Library.

1 3 5 7 9 10 8 6 4 2

ISBN 1 84351 030 8

The Lilliput Press receives financial assistance from
An Chomhairle Ealaíon / The Arts Council of Ireland.

Set in 11.5 on 15.5 Granjon with GillSans display titling
Printed in Ireland by ßetaprint of Dublin

FOREWORD

The story of *Nothing to Say* was written over twenty years ago. At that time I was working as a freelance actor in Dublin's Project Arts Centre, and as a working-class person I was struck by the total lack of stories about contemporary working-class Dublin. Everything seemed to be either about, or for, the middle classes. My class had no voice. Our stories had been hijacked by the college-educated, who patronized and caricatured us.

One morning I was passing a Catholic church. On the ground outside the church lay a crumpled-up body. As I passed, a hand reached out and grabbed my foot. I looked at a face that I barely recognized from childhood. It was a traveller called Johnny, who I'd known in the industrial school. 'Tell them what was done to us,' he said. 'Tell the truth.' And so I began the novel *Nothing to Say*, a story of childhood, one which many people from my background would recognize, as it happened to their children and generations of working-class children before them. Writing the story was frightening: I knew that certain sections of Irish society would reject the notion that the Christian Brothers could do anything wrong. As for the sexual abuse, well, that word was just not heard anywhere in Ireland. Strange, because they all knew that children were being sexually abused by those in authority; the government knew, the police knew, the clergy and religious knew, yet nobody could name it. They were afraid of their own shame, and conspired to deny and hide it.

Nothing to Say is no *Lord of the Flies*; the children in my book do not turn on each other, instead they are savaged by the adults charged with their care. When *Nothing to Say* was first published, many praised my bravery in exposing the inhumanity of the industrial-school system. But I wasn't brave, I wasn't brave enough, I was too frightened. I didn't set out to write a book about abuse or Ireland's industrial and reform school system, I set out to write a book about childhood, to tell as much of the truth as I dared through the eyes of an eleven-year-old character called James O'Neill.

At present, there are continuing criminal investigations into many members of the religious congregations that ran the residential institutions: some have been convicted of horrendous crimes, some still await trial. When they are finally revealed, the stories of unimaginable cruelty by Church and State, and their agents and servants, will haunt this land for a long time to come. Whatever about the crimes of one individual against another, the fact is that the institutions of the Irish State and the Irish Catholic Church enabled and facilitated the mental, emotional, physical and spiritual rape of its most precious charges, its young children.

Twenty years after writing *Nothing to Say* I wrote a play in which the child in *Nothing to Say* has become a man known as James X. He is taking the State to court for the injustices done to him in the industrial and reform schools, the prisons and the mental institutions of Ireland. It is 2002 and as he waits outside the courtroom, James realizes that the Irish courts cannot deliver him justice, only financial compensation. The State offers money to save its soul, with no responsibility, no liability. The Church is still holding onto its toxicity. Faith in God is strong, but the Church is gone. As for me, I hold no grudges. I bear my truth. The truth does set us free, and so does art. Don't repress, express yourself.

GERARD MANNIX FLYNN

August 2003

ACKNOWLEDGMENTS

Aosdána, The Arts Council, Susan Bergin, John Boorman, Liam Carson, the City Arts Centre, Eugene Connolly, Antony Farrell and all at The Lilliput Press, Sandy FitzGerald, Sheridan Flynn, Fubar, The Irish Film Board, Phillippa Kidd, Stephen Kingston, Martin McCann, Ted McCarthy, Niall MacCormack, Philip MacDermott and all at Ward River Press, Declan McGonagle, Annalisa McNamara, Ashlinn McNamara-Flynn, Brian Maguire, Faith O'Grady, Perry Ogden, Sarah Share, Christine Sheridan, South Kerry Partnership, Marsha Swan, Frank T. Zumbach, and my parents and family.

Nothing to Say

ONE

My legs wet, cold water, smell, wake up, sheets? Blankets? Bed. Piss! Ah Jaysus! I'm drowned. 'Here you!' I kicked at my brother at the other end of the bed. 'Wake bleeding up!' No way, all the kicks in the world wouldn't wake him up. I had to get out of the bed. I could feel the piss drying into my shirt and legs. Even me socks were damp. I stumbled in the darkness, trying to open the bedroom door. The handle had been broken so I had to stick my big finger in the hole where the handle was meant to be and pull with all my might. 'You wait,' I said to him as the door flung back, milling into my toe. 'You bastard, I'll get me ma to burst you in the morning.' Out I went, nursing my toe, smelling of piss, to sleep on the settee. There, with me da's topcoat over me, the coals in the grate glowing low, I slept.

Next morning I was screamed at to get over to Keoghs shop on Redmond's Hill and get bread, butter, milk, cornflakes for the breakfast. Half asleep, I stumbled across the main road to the shop which smelled of fig rolls, Kimberlys, Mikados and cream crackers which had been baked in Jacob's. There were a good few people in the shop, including the owners. Two oul' ones and an oul' fella, sisters and brother they were.

'Yes, yes, what do you want, young O'Neill?' said the older woman of the two, at the same time indicating to her brother to get out from behind the counter and watch me.

'Come on now,' she said, getting herself into a hustle and bustle, 'the rest of the customers are waiting.'

'Mmmm, a half-pound of good butter, a batch loaf, two bottles of milk …' I didn't get a chance to say corn – when she barked back at me, 'Did you bring any empties?'

'Na,' I said, and with the next breath telling a big lie, 'me ma's bringing over loads later on.'

She looked at me as if forgetting what she wanted to say next. 'Cornflakes,' I said, 'a big box.'

'Is that the lot?' she asked, taking the cornflakes down from the wooden shelf.

'Yeah.'

Taking the pencil from behind her ear, she made up the prices on the back of the flake box, muttering each item to herself quietly before she had finished writing. Without even looking at me, she held her hand out: 'Ten and twopence.' She looked up when I handed her the pound note, turning away and squinting at it to see if it were real. The sister, who was serving the other people in the shop, peered over her shoulder, assuring her it was a pound. She placed the pound down on the marble top where the tinned beef and cheese lay alongside bags of scattered pennies and ha'pennies, bobs, half-bobs and half-crowns.

Mr Keogh's beady eyes watched me from behind his thick black-framed glasses. Standing there he was, with a look on his face that tried to tell me he wasn't watching me. 'Yes Madam,' he would say to the oul' ones that came into the shop in his let-on posh Switzers accent, 'may I help you?'

'Have you got a cardboard box, Mr Keogh?' I called out,

thinking it would be easier to carry all the messages in. He must be deaf, I thought to myself, after the third time calling him. 'Miss Keogh,' I called to get her attention but there was no go in her either. There she was, getting my change together, examining it like a jeweller would a stone. Every copper she handled, rubbed, and held it at eyelash distance from her eyes, murmuring chant-like 'Ten and two, ten and three, ten and four', and so on, until she reached me proper change.

'I'll be bet around the place when I go back, I'm that long here,' I thought to myself, getting irritated from all the waiting. I started to gather up all the messages from the counter, placing the bread under my arm, the butter in my trousers' pocket, the bottles of milk tightly in my hands and the corn-flakes … Jaysus Christ, there's no way I can carry everything. Maybe I could bring half over to the flat now, then come back for the rest. 'Yeah,' I thought, 'she would be finished counting the change as well and I could get that too.' I was about to go out the door when the other sister, who had stopped serving, asked: 'Where are you going without your cornflakes and your change?'

'I have to go over and come back. I can't carry everything,' I said, my temper rising till I was in the mind to smash the lot of the messages to the floor and run away for good.

'Come here child, could you not ask for a cardboard box?'

I didn't answer her. I watched her disappear out past her brother who I was now convinced stood there asleep with his eyes open. While she was gone, the other one finished the counting of my change from the marble counter into her hand and was now counting it like a snail into my hand. If I had stayed asleep in that pissy bed last night, I would never have had to go for these messages. It was only because I was on that settee and easy prey that Gunner Eyed Martina picked me, her big mouth screaming, 'Get up Humpy and get the messages.'

'One pound, young O'Neill. Well, is that all?' said the oul' one.

'Yeah,' I said, 'but I have to get something to carry the messages in.'

'Will a bag do?' she asked.

I nodded. I turned my back and looked out the door, thinking that it would be like the counting and take ages. I watched the morning buses and cars passing.

'Here,' she said, breaking my concentration, 'there you go.'

'Oh God, now I'll really be bashed.' She had placed all the messages into a paper potato sack. The tears rolled down my face.

'What's wrong? Are you alright?' She put out her hand, trying to lift my face up.

'Me ma will reef me if I bring them home in a sack,' I sobbed, worse now 'cause the oul' one just didn't understand and, to make things even worse, the other sister appeared at her brother's side again, holding a box that was big enough to live in. Like a lunatic, I grabbed the sack and flew out the door. I didn't stop crying nor running until I reached the flights of stone stairs that led to our flat on the second balcony.

Once there, I pulled myself together and, after wiping my face of tears and my nose of snot, I began to take the messages out of the sack and, when I'd wiped them clean of powdery soil, I managed to carry all of them together into the flat.

'Sorry,' I called to Martina, 'that bleedin' Keogh's they never have anythin'. I had to go all the way up Camden Street for butter.' I was wide awake now, as hungry as a seagull, and munching my plate of cornflakes. I took comfort in the thought that I wouldn't have to wash my neck 'cause, as soon as these flakes were eaten and me tea drunk, I was getting me school-bag and sneaking out the door.

There was nobody left in the old tenement houses in York Street. Every day a family would leave, their belongings piled high on the horse and cart, off they would go up to Crumlin or the flats on the Barn. Gangs of us used to scut the cart or run alongside it, cheering all the way up Camden or even further. Mrs Moran was the last to go. I watched as she rode off amid the shouts, catcalls and cheers of all the kids and the good lucks and God bless yous from the other oul' ones that hung out of their windows on the opposite side of the street. 'Giddy up,' said the driver as he tightened his grip on the reins and off she went, heading south to the wide open plains of Crumlin to settle. All that remained now was the sound of water gushing from bursted pipes, the smell of cats and dampness and the never-ending noise of six-inch nails being driven through front hall doors, through galvanized tin and window frames. Imprisoned in their darkness now, the houses remained like bodies left to rot. Months later, men came to pull down what was left.

We all felt bad about that 'cause me, Mucker, Padder and Micko had made a club out of one of the houses and called it the Secko. In it we kept our loft of pigeons, a set of drums and a guitar with no strings. The drums were made from oil cans and boxes but we had real drum sticks. We used to practise there any time we got the chance. Micko was the bloke on guitar. I was the drummer and Padder and Mucker were the fellas that sang the songs. They had to make them up as well. I banged on the drums, Micko made the sounds of the guitar strings from his mouth, while Padder and Mucker gave it all they could.

In our pigeon loft there were two racers, a red and a white, and two gicknas. They didn't know what to make of us. They used to pace up and down the orange box, bumping into each other, flapping their wings and shitting. They never got a second's peace, except for now, the beating of the drums was over and so was our club. The Corporation bulldozers made sure of that. We saved the guitar and the drumsticks as well as the box of pigeons and decided to build a loft in Mucker's ma's pram shed. The days and weeks passed until there was no trace of the old houses and, in their place, two huge car parks. Mucker's oul' fella minded the cars on one of them.

Things didn't go well having the loft in the pram shed. The birds were in the dark all the time and one of us often had to stay with them in case somebody would kill them or Mucker's oul' one would let them out. As well as that, there was loads of slack and coal in the shed and any time you walked on it, coal dust would rise and go all over the pigeons till you couldn't tell which was the red or which was the white. The four of them were black as a blackboard.

It all came to a head one day when I came home from school. I looked for Mucker in the schoolyard that day but he hadn't come in to school so I guessed he'd be minding the birds. After school I was first into the yard of the flats, rushing on in front of me own brothers and sisters and the rest of the kids from our flats. Knock, knock. I waited, my back against the wall of the shed, for the bolt to slide back and let me in. It did and I was in in a flash. Mucker was feeding the birds with corn and bread and they were ploughing into it. It was quiet except for the gurgling from the pigeons. The place was lit with candles from the church at Whitefriar Street. Micko had got them, saying he knew where there was tons. I sat for a while on top of the pile of coal watching Mucker feed. It was not until he moved away to get more corn that I noticed there was one pigeon gone and something told me it wasn't bleedin' mine.

'What happened to the other pigeon?' I asked.

'I had him out of the box and he flew off,' said Mucker, letting slip the slight sound of a snigger.

'Whose pigeon was it?' I asked, knowing full well it was his.

'It was yours.'

Mucker burst out laughing, falling about the place. I stood up to look into the orange box to check, but you couldn't tell which was which 'cause they were still black with the dirt. Mucker's laughing was getting on my nerves. I wanted to split him open with a lump of coal to stop his jeering laughter. In an instant I slapped back the bolt, grabbed the box of birds and, before Mucker could catch his breath, I was off, heading fast up the stairs towards the flat. But Mucker was faster. I only made it to the first landing. I halted dead in my tracks, screaming, 'If you come up, I'll dump them over the balcony. I'm warning ya.'

Mucker's face was red with temper, his tongue hung out the side of his mouth, his fists waving in the air.

'Yer dead,' he called, 'I swear on me ma's life, yer dead if ya kill them racers. Now you'd better give them back.'

'No, my bird was red and this is it. It was your own bird you let out.' He tried to move towards the stairs. 'I'm telling ya, I'll smash the lot of them down into the square. Don't move.'

He was biting his tongue like a dog bites a bone, tears running down his cheeks. 'Please, I'll pay ya for them ...'

Before he could get the rest of what he was saying out, I said 'No,' and at the same time, made a move to dump the box of birds over the balcony. It worked. He ran out of the way enough to give me a good start up the stairs. With Mucker hard on my heels, I got to my hall door. It was locked. The pigeons were squeaking and squawking, terrified out of their wits, flapping about madly, trapped inside their orange box. I booted, banged, bet the knocker till it nearly came off in my hand.

'Martina! Martina!' I screamed through the letter-box in total panic. 'Open the door. Mucker Liddy is trying to rob me box of birds.'

Mucker was now facing me, sucking in air like a raging bull. It frightened me. 'Ma, Ma, me ma's coming out. See will you take the pigeons then!' I was pressed hard up against the hall door, trapped, hoping that someone would open the door.

'Hold on one moment now, James, and I'll give it to you. Me bit of a home is bad enough without you starting to kick down the door ...' Before she'd finished her sentence, the door was open and I fell into the hall.

'Ma, Ma, Mucker is trying to rob the pigeons that I bought. He said he's going to batter me, I swear,' I said, making the sign of the cross with my finger on my Adam's apple.

'Is that so, now?' said me ma to Mucker, who was standing outside the door making fists at me.

'Mrs O'Neill,' sobbed Mucker, 'I swear on me granny's grave that I may drop dead right now, James is after robbing those birds on me out of me ma's pram shed. His own pigeon flew away.'

'Ma, don't mind him. My bird was red and his was white and the one that I have here is red. The white one was his and he let it out himself, didn't ya,' I roared out at him from behind me ma, 'an' now he's tryin' to say it's mine.'

'Mrs O'Neill, I'm going to get him in school tomorrow and dance on him,' cried Mucker, as he headed towards the stairs, 'I swear that on me granny's grave,' holding out both his hands and closing his eyes as if summoning up the dead. 'I swear

James, I swear.' And off he went in convulsions up to his flat on the top balcony.

Before I had time to breathe a sigh of relief, me ma's hand came tumbling down into the back of me neck. 'Get in there ya trouble-rising bastard. Get yourself into bed and these poor birds out of that box.'

'Ah Ma, please let's keep them,' I cried.

'I told you you're not keeping poor birds like that in this flat. You'll have the wrath of Jaysus on the place. Now I'm warning you for the last time, get those birds out before yer father comes in from work, before they louse up the house.'

'Ah go on Ma. Let them stay in the coal-box in the hall.' The tears that were falling down off my face were splashing in through the slats of the orange box and onto the pigeons. 'Go on Ma, will ya? Will ya?'

'Alright, stop your whinging. Give them a bit of bread and leave them there in the coal-box till your father comes in. Now, shut up that trouble-rising mouth of yours 'cause if you don't, them pigeons are getting booted out.'

It wasn't long until all my younger brothers and sisters charged through the door and into the sitting-room demanding at the top of their voices: 'Hey Ma, what's for dinner?' 'Chips, eggs and beans,' came the reply. 'Ah Ma, I don't luyke eggs,' stuttered Pauline. 'Ma, I'll eat her eggs,' said Anthony. 'Never mind who's going to eat the eggs. Sit Thomas and Marian up at the table and feed them their dinner,' said me ma. Within a short while everybody was at the table with their dinner. The red sauce was passed around and emptied onto the chips. So was the vinegar, and the salt was everywhere bar on the dinner. Glass after glass of milk was drank with the exception of the odd one, two or three being spilt. You could tell when one was about to go and you moved out of the way. It would be all over the table, all over the chairs and forming little white puddles on the lino-covered floor. Me da said that you'd be better off sitting under the table with your mouth open. 'Ye'd have a better chance of getting milk,' he said.

After wiping the spilt milk off the floor I brought the floor-cloth out to the toilet to squeeze it into the bowl. There must have been about two pints in it. I watched the water in the bowl go white like when you pour Jeyes Fluid in. It looked kind of nice so I didn't flush the chain. Instead I crept out to the coal-box in the hall and had a look at the pigeons to see if they were alright. 'How are yez? Tweet, tweet,' I whistled. 'Did yez not eat your bread?' I placed my finger in between the slats of the box to rub one of the birds. They got frightened and started flapping and squawking about the cage. 'It's alright, don't worry,' I pulled my finger out of the box in the hope that it would shut them up. No such thing. They got worse and before I could cover the box up, the sitting-room door opened and there were two of my brothers, Brian and Anthony.

'Where'd you get the birds?' asked Brian.

'Got a lend of them. They're not mine,' I said, trying to push them back into the sitting-room.

'I'm telling me ma if you push me again,' snapped Anthony. 'She bleedin' knows they're here.'

'Then let us feed them will ya?' Anthony pleaded. 'OK,' I said, 'but only youse two and only give them little bits.'

There was no stopping them. Anything that was on the plates was dumped in on top of the birds. Eggs, chips, beans, red sauce. Soon it got to total mayhem with Pauline crying, terrified of the birds, and me gone off the rocker. 'They don't eat chips, ya stupid swine ya.' 'What's going on out there?' Me ma's voice called from the kitchen. 'James, are you at it again?

I hope you're not battering those children.'

Next thing, she's out of the kitchen and beside the gang of us. 'Who did that to God's poor creatures?' she asked with pity in her voice. Everybody pointed at everybody else. I looked down at the pigeons, sobbing, 'Look what they done, Ma. They did that,' I said, pointing my finger at Anthony and Brian. Before she even clattered them, they were off crying and saying, 'We didn't mean to, Ma, honest, we didn't.'

'I told you about those pigeons, James.' Me ma was in a temper now. 'I told you that they would bring God's wrath upon this flat. Now, I want them birds out of here now, ya fucking swine. You just wait till your father comes in.'

The thought of having to get rid of my birds was nearly the death of me. 'I'm not bleeding doing it,' I screamed at her.

'Right, now, I'll give you pigeons.'

'Ma, don't!' It was no use. The box was open. 'Anthony,' she called. 'Open that hall door.'

I was crying, sobbing. In a last-ditch effort to prevent the release of my birds, I dived towards the hall door, but on my way, in full panic, I tripped over the box which fell over onto its side, spilling out the pigeons, which in turn took flight towards the locked windows. I tried to call one of the birds down from the lampshade while me ma calmed the younger kids, Thomas and Marian, who had gone into fits of convulsions from fear of the terrified pigeons. It became useless. Any time I got near the birds, off they would go, bashing into walls and windows. Then everyone would start screaming as if the pigeons were going to bleeding eat them. 'Are you going to open that window, James?' said me ma, clutching the two youngest who seemed a little bit calmer.

'Can't let them out now Ma, 'cause they're hurt,' I said, creeping up on one of the birds who could not fly. 'Got ya.' I threw my coat over him. 'I have one, Ma.' There was two more and now Anthony and Brian were helping me. Brian was swiping his jumper at the one that stood on the lampshade. It was not long till we had him back into the box but, before we could get the last one, me ma pulled down the window, whooshed the bird, and off he went. We all ran to the window to say goodbye.

'There he is Ma, look, he's a great flyer,' I said. 'Quick Ma, before he goes.' She never came over near the window. The kids weren't frightened anymore and my red bird that got turned black from the coal dust was now back red, covered in tomato sauce, flying through the air.

'Right,' says me ma, 'James, put that box of pigeons out on top of the coal-box and take these two children down into the yard and mind them until I call you. Anthony, get up to Camden Street and get me half a stone of potatoes, carrots, parsley and onions. Thomas, shut up you crying bastard, the birds are gone.'

'Hey Ma,' I said. 'Mucker Liddy might get me if I go down into the yard.'

'If any of the Liddys puts a hand on you, you just come up here to me. We're not afraid of them or anyone like them. Go on now, off you go, and James, you better not leave those children.'

The kids played in the yard and I watched over them, warning them every few minutes not to go out of the gate. I also kept me eye on Mucker's front hall door 'cause I knew that he was bound to attack and I had to be ready to scream to me ma for help. Between the kids trying to scarper out of the flats and watching for Mucker's door to open, I got fed up with the boredom of not being able to play myself. I didn't notice the door of Mucker's pram shed opening nor had I time to duck the lump of coal that bounced off my head, spilling blood down my face and dripping down off my jumper. It wasn't until the blood splashed onto the ground that I realized I was split open. It felt as if time had stopped, the only thing I could feel was the warmth of the blood on my face. The kids in the flats all gathered around me, their voices saying, 'Oh looket, he's bleedin'.' 'Oh Holy God, yer gushing.' 'There's all blood on ya.' 'Tell his ma.'

I ran all wet and sticky up the stairs towards me flat, banged the door as hard as I could. 'Ma, Ma, I'm split open, Ma, I'm bleeding split,' I shouted. The door opened. 'Oh Jaysus!' said me ma, falling against the wall of the hall, her hands reaching to cover her eyes. Within seconds the hall was covered in little red spots. 'Ma, Mucker Liddy did it. He's gone running out of the flats,' I said.

Without any more delay she wrapped a towel that smelt of soap around my head, whipped on her coat and scarf and in no time had me at Mercer's Hospital where the nurses washed my hair and asked me, 'Do you have a girlfriend?' and, 'Aren't you great not to be crying?' The doctors came to look at me and asked, 'What happened to you?' 'Mucker Liddy split me with a lump of coal,' I said. 'Is that so, well he must be a naughty bold boy. Tell me now if this hurts.' I could feel the hands of the doctor pressing down on me head. 'Na,' I said.

He moved away from me over towards where a long silver pot was boiling. I watched him push his fingers into the rubber gloves and then I really started to get frightened at the knives and things like pincers, needles and all that the nurse was taking out of the pot. The steam billowed and I could even hear the water bubbling. The nurse looked over at me and smiled. 'You're the bravest little boy that we have ever had. How old are you?'

'I'm nearly eleven,' I said.

The doctor picked up the syringe, placed the needle into it. I watched him stick the needle into a small bottle, the bottle drained as the syringe sucked. Now the syringe was full with it. Too much maybe 'cause he squirted some of it out into the air and I could get the smell of it. Desperate it was. 'Come along with me James,' said the nurse. She slid back a yellow-covered door, pointed to a bed which had big bottles that were made of steel. I knew what they were 'cause I had seen them on the telly and in garages. I looked at the clocks that were on top of them and the tubes that hung from either side.

The nurse said, 'Hop up there on that nice comfy bed for me, will you.' I did. 'There's a good man,' she said. She moved out of my line of vision and I saw the doctor with the syringe in his hand and a white mask over his face.

'Ma, Ma,' I cried.

'Now, now, we're not going to hurt you, just a little prick and it will be over.'

'Ma, Ma, com'ere!'

It was no use. The nurse sat on the side of the bed and the doctor, with the nurse holding me down, stuck the needle into me head. It didn't really hurt, but I didn't stop me crying until me ma came in asking, 'Will he be kept in?' 'No, not at all. There's no need,' I heard the doctor say. 'Now, now, it's all over,' said the nurse. 'There, that wasn't too bad now, was it?' 'No, it was alright,' I said. 'Well, I'll just put a dressing on it and you can be off with your friends.'

The dressing was done in a minute. I stood beside me ma with a bandage that was as big as a blanket wrapped around me head. The doctor spoke to my mother, telling her that if I got sick or dizzy pains in the head or anything of that nature, to come straight back and not to forget to bring me back next week for a change of bandage. Me ma thanked the nurse and the doctor, took me by the hand out of the hospital and straight into Peter's Pub across the road, ordered a bottle of stout for herself, crisps and orange for me. There we both sat for the rest of the afternoon not saying very much to each other. We left at about half-five, me ma telling me to run on home, placing two bob in my hand, saying, 'I'm going off on a message.' 'OK Ma,' I said. She headed off and I headed for the shops for another packet of Tayto.

Before I reached the gate of the flats, I had finished off the packet of Tayto. Outside the gate, I wiped me mouth and in I went, not forgetting to pick up a stone just in case Mucker might be around the corner. He was there alright, on the top balcony with his ma, well out of reach. I looked up at him but he took no notice of me, maybe because he didn't recognize me with the big bandage on me head. Me ma will get him, I thought, as I reached the first step of the stone stairs that led to our flat. I was on the second landing when I saw the DSPCA van come into the flats. I waited there, watching it stop and a man got out. 'Who are ya looking for Mister?' I called. He didn't answer. He was checking the numbers on the hall doors. Next thing I hear Martina's voice, 'Here Mister, up here, come on up and get them.' The pigeons, I thought, she's getting rid of me pigeons. I ran up the stairs, but when I got to the house it was useless. Me da had come home from work and he stood now at the hall door, holding the orange box of pigeons.

'Ah Da, don't. Let's keep the birds, please,' I said, whimpering.

'Me ma said that those birds were to go 'cause they're full of disease,' snarled Martina, 'They have brought nothing but trouble since they were brought in here by you. Even Mrs Liddy is after being down here fightin' over them, so they're

25

bleeding goin' and that's that.'

I cried, cursing Mucker Liddy, Gunner-Eyed Martina and the man from the DSPCA who was taking me pigeons away in a van.

Me, me da and me sister watched over the balcony as the van doors were opened. Lots of kids had gathered round the man with the pigeons, asking, 'Ah go on Mister, give us them, will ya? See can they fly still.' The man didn't answer. In the birds went and the door slammed shut. Then the man spoke, 'Come along now, out of the way from the van.' Then he got in behind the wheel and rolled down the window. 'Come on, come on out of the way or you'll get knocked down.'

'Here you,' said Martina to me, 'get in, your tea's ready.'

'Wait, will you,' I replied. I took my last look as the van left the flats, with the kids hanging on the back trying to open the back door. 'Come on,' she said again.

'Alright,' said I, wiping the tears and the snot off my face. 'I'm coming, I'm bleeding coming.'

TWO

There were fourteen of us as well as me ma and da. The eldest was a girl, May. Then came Sue, Martina, Barbara, Angela, then Liam, who died, then I came along, and after me came Anthony, Brian, Pauline, Christopher, Johnny, Charley, Thomas and Marian. Our flat had two rooms for sleeping, a toilet, a sitting-room and a kitchen with a bath plumbed into the corner. You had to queue for everything in our flat and fights often broke out, rows about somebody wearing somebody else's clothes.

The police called to our flats often and when they did, it was more than likely to the O'Neills'. My mother and father would start fighting and screaming at each other. The next-door neighbour would come in and try and stop them. Then, when the fight was over, my mother would call the police and want them to keep Da from the house. But the police knew it was the same old story. They would say a few words and then leave.

My father would often leave and go to live in a men's hostel. We would see him most days coming home from work because he drank in Falvey's pub, and every Friday one of the family would have to go to the pub and get me ma's money, four pounds. Four pounds and whatever me ma made selling fruit and veg from her stall in Camden Street got us by OK. My sister Sue also brought us over clothes and money. She had left home at about fourteen years of age and gotten into all sorts of trouble. She didn't give a fuck what anybody said about what she did – she went from shop to shop, from police station to police station, from court to court and from prison to prison and back again.

I remember the time she had a baby. The house was in up-roar. My mother kept the baby and reared it. The baby was a boy called Charley. I think Sue was happy enough to let Ma look after him. Sue hung around with a girl called Mag King and there wasn't a shop nor police station that didn't know the two of them. My other sisters were working in factories. Some-times Sue would take May, the eldest sister, out drinking and dancing.

One Easter me ma had bought us all Easter eggs. It was about eight o'clock and May was minding the house while Ma was in the pub. May had just given us all a bath and we were going to bed. I didn't want to go to bed but I was put in any-way, so I kept all the other kids awake fighting with them. Then the bedroom door burst open and in came May. She clat-ters me into bed, puts a pillow over my head and sits on me. I slept after that.

Next morning we all woke mad for our Easter eggs. Out of bed like lightning and into the sitting-room. There they were, all lined up on top of the sideboard, my eyes going from one to the other to see which was the biggest. I didn't get a chance to look at them all. The rest of the kids were coming out of the bedroom like a herd of cattle on stampede. As far as I could see all the Easter eggs were the same size. So I grabbed my egg, any egg, and the rest of the kids grabbed theirs. Wrappers and cartons were ripped apart in no time and hands, mouths, floor and chairs were jam-caked with chocolate. I started to open my egg, opening the carton, being careful not to spill out any of the milk choc buttons that were inside. I took the egg out of the box and nearly burst into tears. The whole back of the Easter egg had been eaten away. Tears began to run down my face with temper. I thought to myself, that dirty fat pig could not wait to get us into bed last night and then, when she did, the sleveen opened the boxes on the eggs and ate the back off them, put the eggs back into the boxes and placed them nice and neat on the sideboard.

It was at one of the dances that Sue brought May to that May met her boyfriend, Kevin Coleman. I remember the two of them often used to sit on the steps of the flats kissing. Eventually they ran away to get married. I remember one night there was a knock at the door and it was Punchy Quinn, a friend of Kevin Coleman's.

'Is your mother in?' he said.

'Yeah, hold on a minnut,' I said, calling Ma.

'What's up?' she said. 'Is there something wrong?'

I was pushed back into the sitting-room. The next thing I heard was 'married …' and 'Where are they going to live?' My mother came back into the sitting-room, got her coat and was gone out the door.

Later on that night there was a big hooley in the flat. I was asleep in bed and was woken up by all the singing that was going on. I got up and went into the sitting-room, for I was sure to make a few bob, and I did. Kevin and May gave me a load but it wasn't till early in the morning that it hit me why they gave me so much money. It was their cold feet that woke me, and there they were, the newly-weds, sleeping down the bottom of my bed.

Most days me and a friend, Eamon Doyle, used to go on the mitch. We would meet in St Patrick's Park in Bride Street and go off for the day, up along the canal to the Dogs and Cats Home. We would have a good look at the dogs, petting them, feeding them and all the time trying to find a way to open the cages and let them out. But in the back of my mind, I couldn't help thinking about the vicious dogs, the ones that had gone mad. If you let one out, you had to let them all out, and I was fucked if I was letting any mad dog out to bite the bleeding arse off me. Then off we'd go down to Bolands Mills for our cakes. We'd sneak into where they loaded up the vans, stuff our jumpers with goodies and get out the gate hanging off the back of the van.

We used to go everywhere – Blackrock, Bray, shops, parks, everywhere but school, and when we would get tired from walking, we'd go up to Jacob's factory and get ourselves two bicycles and off we'd go again. We were mad for bikes. One time, me da brought home two three-wheel bikes that he had found in the dump. One of the bikes had only two wheels, and the other had no chain. Me da got this great idea. He put the bike that had only two wheels into the back of the one that had three. I think the O'Neills of Connolly House were the first kids in the world to have a five-wheeler bike. It carried everybody.

I never liked going to school, they'd be lucky to see me at school for half an hour. My sister, Martina, who minded the family, used to bring me by the scruff of the neck to school any morning she could, but more times, I would break free of her grip and have it off on my toes. And if I could not break free then I'd wait my chance and get over the school wall, bringing half a dozen others with me. There were about forty of us in the class and the Master said that most of us had more nits than brains. The odd time that I was in school the Master would call me up to the front of the class and in a high voice, he'd say: 'I-2-3-4-5-6-7, all good children go to Heaven; I-2-3-4-5-6-7, all bad boys go to Letterfrack.' I thought he was a madman, but I soon found out that what he was saying was true.

The day that I got sent to Letterfrack my ma came with me to the court. I was all nice and clean in new shoes and new clothes. That morning was like any other morning. The Corpo were cleaning out the chutes, and all the kids were in school. Passing down Aungier Street, people from the flats would stop us and say, 'God help you, Kathleen. Your heart must be broke going in and out of courts. I don't blame you getting drunk, but God is good. Maybe he'll learn his lesson and be a good boy.' My mother never paid any attention to what they were saying for they never stopped reporting our family to the Corpo, and couldn't wait to see the back of me. Me ma used to always let me smoke when I was going to court.

The court was in the lower yard of Dublin Castle and there was a waiting-room on the left as you went in the door. The first person I saw as I entered the building was the School Inspector who nodded to me and said 'Hello' to me ma. Ma brought me into the waiting-room. Everybody there knew everybody else. All the ma's sat and talked together, while we, like children in a play-pen, scribbled our case histories on walls, doors and floors. Some drew girls with tits as big as weather balloons. Between the smoking and the scribbling, everybody was on edge, nervous and frightened. Case after case was called, every mother wishing the others all the best as they climbed the stairs holding the hands of their children tightly. Every now and again the courts would go into uproar as some boy got sent down and the cop took him from his crying mother down to the cell.

The charges I had to answer were for non-attendance at school, the larceny of a bicycle and possession of stolen toys. I was called: Garda Kennedy and James O'Neill. I put out my cig, took a deep breath and climbed the steps, getting more and more frightened.

I had been warned by the Judge before that if she saw me again in her court she would send me away. 'Run,' I thought to myself, 'have it in your toes, don't be a fool. Your last chance, don't throw it away.' I was caught between fear of escaping and the thought of Letterfrack. My mother's face looked pained and drawn. A woman was standing at the top of the steps with a prayer book in her hand. It was the woman who owned the push-bike I had been charged with taking. She was an oldish woman with a religious face.

The courtroom was painted in bright colours. To the left as you came in the door were two big windows with net curtains. There were a lot of benches leading straight up to the press bench. Next came the Judge's bench. To the left of her sat the Probation Officer. To the right sat the Court Clerk. My mother sat on the public benches as did the woman with the prayer book. The School Inspector sat in one of the witness benches and the policeman sat up the back of the court with some other cops. I was brought down to the front of the court and placed beside a big open fireplace. On top of the fireplace there was a big long wooden clock.

I looked up at the Judge with a smile on my brain that could not get onto my face. She looked down at me. My hands were getting cold and wet. I felt awkward, uneasy and more and more afraid. Again the thought of escaping was lashing at my brain. I could run across the courtroom and dive through one of the big windows. Time was running out, so were my chances of escape.

The first charge to be called was the larceny of the push-bike. The Court Clerk read the charge sheet out, 'James O'Neill, that you, the said accused, did between the times and the dates set out on Pearse Street sheet number 94 in the Dublin Metropolitan District feloniously without the owner's consent steal one lady's bicycle valued at 30 shillings, the property of Mrs Roe, 190 Pembroke Street, and that you the said accused had in your possession one push-bike known to have been stolen. Furthermore, on that same date, you had in your possession other property known to have been stolen, two Dinky toys valued at two shillings, the property of Kevin Melia, Werburgh Street. You understand the charges before you. Guilty or not guilty?' Again I looked at the Judge and replied: 'Guilty, Your Honour.' She wrote the reply into her book. I looked back to my mother, she tried to smile at me. My heart began to pound in my chest. I was fighting now to stop my tears.

Now came the charge of non-attendance at school. The School Inspector took the witness stand and read out my school record. He said I hadn't been at school for months and that when I did show up I was troublesome. He also stated that I had been in court before for non-attendance at school and that I could not read nor write.

The Judge turned to me and asked had I anything to say as to why I hadn't been to school. I told her I had nothing to say. The Judge then turned to my mother.

'Mrs O'Neill, have you anything to say in relation to this matter?'

My mother rose to her feet and said: 'Yes, Your Honour. I kept him from school myself, because I need him to help me at home and to bring the stalls up to the street.' The Judge said she had heard this all before and said it was no excuse. My mother said that she was very sick and needed someone to help her with the younger children.

'I cannot let this boy run wild around the streets of Dublin when he should be in school learning and getting an education. What use will he be when he grows up not being able to read nor write?'

Ma was crying, weeping, asking for another chance for me, swearing that she herself would take me to school every morning and that I wouldn't miss another day.

'Mrs O'Neill,' said the Judge, 'you say you are a sick woman. You have other children who need looking after. You cannot spend your life running around after James.'

The Probation Officer took the stand, Miss Leahy. She said that I was a disturbed and unruly child. That there was a drink problem in the home and frequent separations, that the housing situation was bad. Me ma was still crying. The people in the courtroom were quiet. I could feel the atmosphere in the room. I knew what was coming now and began to make myself ready for it.

The Judge turned to me and said, 'James O'Neill, you have been convicted on all counts before this court and I'm committing you to St Joseph's Industrial School until you are fourteen. You will go to school now.'

Now I could feel nothing in my body. I wanted to piss, get sick and shit all at the same time.

A hand went tightly around my wrist. It got tighter and tighter as we moved towards the door.

'You cunt,' my mother screamed at the Judge, 'what do you know about children, you're nothing but a fucking empty vessel.' Then, her voice getting louder and louder, she turned on the Probation Officer. I looked up into me ma's eyes. They were roaring red. Her face was wet from tears. She used her scarf to wipe the tears away. I stopped dead in my tracks and turned right around to face the Judge, staring her in the eyes with every bit of hatred I could muster. My mother was still crying and screaming as the policemen tried to remove her from the courtroom. The cop who had my hand was getting edgy and started to pull at me. We moved out of the courtroom and down the stairs. At the bottom of the stairs there were more policemen. Somebody called out, 'Leave the child alone, youse bastards,' at the policemen, while another said with pity, 'God bless you son.'

I was searched and told to empty my pockets. They gave me back my cigs and some other stuff. I just looked at them all the time, not saying anything, trying to tell them without saying it that I didn't care if they locked me up on the moon or if I never saw the light of day again. If I had tried to say anything, I just would have broke up and cried my heart out, but I was not going to let them see me do that.

The cell was a large room with two big windows with bars, mesh wire and plastic glass. It also had a big bench which was nailed to the floor.

The cell door closed behind me as quickly as it had been opened. As soon as it did, some of the other boys in the cell with me ran over to the wire mesh opening in the door and called after the policemen: 'Your wife's a big ride, youse red-neck bastards. Hey, mallet head, you're a bent pig.' I went over and sat on the long wooden seat, trying to think but could not. 'How long did you get?' somebody called over to me. 'Six years in Letterfrack,'; 'What copper had you up?'; 'Kennedy's an oul' dog,'; 'Where you from?'; 'Do you know Peter Bracken?'; 'You ever up before?'; 'What were you nicked for?'; 'What sta-

tion had you?'; 'Do you wanna smoke?'; 'Letterfrack's a kip.'
The questions went on and on.

My eyes roamed around the walls of the cell which were
full of names, numbers, dates and sentences: 'Martin 3 years 6
months', 'Micka 6 months', 'Shay McGowan no bail – aged 9',
'Kevin aged 8', 'Batman was here for Robin', and in big black
marker was written, 'You'll do it on your ear'.

The other boys walked up and down the cell, kicked the
door and looked for space on the wall to write their names.
The cell was cold and dirty; light from the outside did its best
to break through the dirty windows. I sat on the seat and
smoked. The smoke drifted like a fog around the cell and,
when the door was opened, it seemed to make a mad charge
to get out. Me ma came into the cell with a paper bag in her
hand. She gave the bag to me and kissed me on the cheek. Inside the bag was cigs, matches, chocolate, sweets, fruit and a
bottle of coke. We didn't say anything. I drank some coke and
so did my mother. Then she gave some to the other boys. The
tears began to roll down my mother's face. I sat, half-embar-
rassed because the other boys were watching. I didn't know
where to look or what to do. I looked at the ground so nobody
would see my face. I wanted to cry so much but I wanted to be
a hard man too, and caught between the two, my heart just
bursted. My eyes filled with water. The tears ran down my
face like blood from a wound and spilled onto the floor. My
ma put her arms around me and told me not to worry, that she
would make an appeal and get me out on bail. As the tears
poured out and the sobs went on, I began to feel relaxed, that
I had released something. I took out my cigs, gave me ma one
and had one myself. One of the boys came over and gave us a
light. He was about fifteen.

'Letterfrack is not all that bad,' he said, 'you get used to it after a while and there are a lot worse bleeding places. Just keep out of trouble and you'll be alright.' My mother gave him a cig and asked him what he was in for. 'Bleeding everything,' he replied. 'I'm going up to Marlborough House on remand.' He left and went back to his friends, giving one of them the butt-end of his cig. My tears stopped now and I could hear the rattle of keys outside the cell door. The door opened. A load of policemen were standing outside.

'Come on now, lads, or you'll be late for your tea.'

The older boys moved to the door quickly, as if they were going to make a run for it. The cops got panicky. As the gang got to the door, they turned right around and walked back into the cell, falling about the place laughing.

I stood with my parcel in my arms, hugging me ma and telling her not to worry. My mother left the cell first. I could hear her crying as she left. I moved towards the door. One of the policemen got hold of my wrist like a pair of tight handcuffs. There was a policeman for every two steps I took. People were watching me. I felt strange not knowing what to do with myself. I felt that they were pitying me, saying, 'God help him.' I threw a few shapes for the benefit of the onlookers, but it didn't work. I was a child and that was that.

The Black Maria was parked outside the courthouse, its back doors wide open. It was one of those transit vans and it had windows all along both sides of it. There were seats inside something like a minibus. I was put into the van and Kennedy and another policeman got in with me. The doors of the van were shut tight. The engine started up. Some of the people who were inside the court-house watched us go off. As we moved, I took a look out of the window. Me ma was standing on the footpath. She gave me a slight smile and I waved back at her full of sadness. I was crying inside.

THREE

The Black Maria drove through the streets of Dublin. I knew that this was my last look. I was kind of hoping that I might see someone that I knew and then I could wave to them or scream out the window at them. But it was a quiet journey except in my head. Smoking and thinking, thinking and hoping, hoping and praying, praying and crying.

It must have been twelve o'clock when the Black Maria stopped at the train station. I could hear the Angelus ringing. Garda Kennedy blessed himself, I did too. The driver opened my door and took hold of my hand tightly. With one cop holding my hand and the other closely by my side, we moved into the station office. People were moving everywhere, carrying bags, getting on trains, off trains. I was beginning to liven up and be myself again. People were looking over at me, trying to figure out why the cop had me. I put on a 'doesn't bother me' look. The cop handed some documents to the man in the office, and the man stamped them and told us the time of the train. It must have looked funny to the people watching us as we walked down the platform. I was in the middle, the two huge policemen, one on each side, holding my hands.

We reached the train and got on. The driver of the police

van left us. Kennedy put me into the seat beside the window and sat in the aisle seat beside me.

I looked out the window, thinking, remembering the time my da took half the family to the seaside. The platform was packed with people and my sister Angela held me by the hand, in case I might get lost. As the train came into the station, there was a big mad rush for it. Me and my sister were pushed forward by the crowds. I got frightened, thinking that we were going to be killed by the train. I began to cry. So did Angela. Angela called out for me da. Just as the train stopped, me da had caught hold of us and we were safe. Then he got into bad humour and started giving out to us. Anyway, we started to get onto the train. We were all on board when Angela told me da that she had lost her good shoe. It had come loose as she was getting on the train. Me da started to curse and swear. 'You could not bring youse nowhere, youse could not be taken into the jungle.' We all had to get off the train and look for the shoe. We all spread out and looked up and down the platform. It was nowhere to be seen. Then Angela said, 'There it is, Da.' We all moved over to where Angela was standing. The shoe was lying between the train and the platform wall. Da told us to go and sit down. We all sat for a while, then the train began to pull out of the station and I began to cry 'cause I thought that me da was going to bring us all back home. Then everybody began to give out to Angela. 'It's all your fault, you dopey, stupid eejit.' Da was still on the platform looking at the shoe lying on the track. On the seat, we were ready to throw Angela in front of the next train. Da got down onto the track and got the shoe, brought it back to Angela and told her to put it on.

We sat for a while until the next train came along. Me da gave us some of our seaside sandwiches to keep us quiet. The train pulled into the station. Me da had us all on in a flash and we were away.

Sitting beside Kennedy on the train brought that day back to me. The journey seemed to pass quite slowly. Maybe because the train stopped almost everywhere, and any time it stopped, I thought that we were there – wherever we were supposed to be. I was beginning to get uneasy sitting in the seat all the time. I wanted to get up and have a look around the train. Kennedy began to notice this and asked did I want to go to the toilet. 'Yes,' I said. He got up from his seat and took me by the hand to the toilet. He stood outside until I had finished. Every few seconds he would knock on the toilet door and ask was I alright. He didn't give a bollix whether I was alright or all wrong as long as I wasn't getting out the bleeding window. Anyhow I couldn't get the window open, so out I came again. Back in my seat, I noticed people were looking at me in a kind of funny way. They had that pitying look on their faces.

We passed more rivers. There was one big one with boats on it. The morning got brighter and brighter. As we moved along I could see the sun trying to break through the clouds and I was beginning to feel hot and sticky. The cop bought me a bottle of lemonade and gave me twenty cigs. He broke the monotony for a while by asking me about my family. Then he talked about Letterfrack.

'Well, at least you'll come out with a trade.'

The man came up the carriage checking the tickets. When it came to our turn, Kennedy handed him a piece of paper. The man read it and handed it back. I could feel him looking at me for a while.

I smoked. The cop smoked. The passengers smoked. The train passed station after station, field after field, bridge after bridge, going fast, going slow, people getting on and getting off, pushing and shoving, hurrying and rushing. I looked out the window for a good while, no thoughts going through my head, just my eyes taking it all in, not being able to understand this strange adventure. I stared out the window and Kennedy stared at me. After a while I got a pain in me bollix looking out the window all the time, so I asked would there be anybody to meet us at the train station.

'There'll be a Brother to meet you at Galway Station, and he'll bring you to Letterfrack,' Kennedy said.

'Will you not be coming down to Letterfrack with us?' I asked.

'No, I leave you in Galway and I go back up to Dublin. Sure, you'll be back up in Dublin yourself in six months' time, if you keep yourself out of trouble.'

'What do you mean?'

'Well, the Brothers let you home for a holiday.'

I could see that he was trying to be nice to me, and I began to think of what a bastard he was, going around the flats on his police Triumph motorbike, chasing me on the lady's push-bike all around the kip.

The day that he lagged me, I was coming out of the flats doing about fifteen to twenty miles an hour. I just passed York Street going towards Mercer's Hill, when I heard the engine of the police bike and Kennedy's voice saying, 'Come here, James. I want to talk to you.' 'Yeah,' I said to myself, 'so does the FBI.' Looking around, I could see him at the top of York Street. I was really going fast now. The push-bike sped down Mercer's Hill and I just kept on peddling. The wind was lashing against my face and the mud-guards began to rattle and make a lot of noise. On down past Mercer's Hospital and into South William Street. The cop was coming up behind me. At the top of William Street, I was right bollixed. I had to stop.

I pulled into the side of the path. So did Kennedy. He got off his bike, keeping his eye on me all the time. 'Well, James, who owns the bike?'

'I found it in the flats, but I think my sister owns it.'

'Which sister?'

'Me sister Martina.'

'And what would she be doing with a bike?'

'Don't know,' I said.

'Well,' the cop said, 'I'll have to take you down to the station, because there's a woman there who says that the bike is hers, and she is not your sister, so we'll soon find out who owns the bike.'

He called me over to his side, then he radioed headquarters for a car to take me to the cop-shop. Kennedy asked me again and again where I got the bike.

'I told you where I got it,' I kept saying.

A crowd from the flats began to gather on the street, gawking at the two of us. 'You'd think the child was after robbing a bank the way you have him,' a woman called out to the copper. 'Someone run up and get his mother.' The police car came and took me to the cop-shop.

The train began to slow down and Kennedy stopped talking to me. People began to take their bags down off the shelves, put on their coats and sit down again. Slowly, slowly, and the train stopped.

'This is it, James,' said Kennedy.

I got up to go but Kennedy told me to sit back until the rest of the people had got off. When we got down onto the platform he held me by the hand again and we strolled over to the main entrance. The sun was blazing in the sky as we came out of the train station. The place was packed with people, cars beeping at each other. My hand was getting sore from him holding it too tight. I told him and he held me by the wrist instead. We walked up and down the path. Kennedy was looking for the Brother that was to meet us. I was hoping that he wouldn't turn up. That Kennedy would have to bring me back home.

A green car pulled up beside us and a Brother got out with a smile on his face.

'Hello, hello. Were you waiting long? Sorry, I'm Brother McCann from St Joseph's School.' The Brother shook both our hands.

'This is James O'Neill, Brother. The lad from Dublin,' said the cop. 'A fine lad he is too.'

'There you go, James,' said the Brother, opening the door of the car. 'Sit in there for a while. I'll be with you in a minute.'

I sat in the car for a while. I could see Kennedy give the Brother some papers and a big envelope. Then they came over to the car. The Brother got into the driver's seat and Kennedy came to my door and opened it. He gave me his hand. I looked at it and gave him mine.

'Well, James. Good luck to you and take care of yourself.'

Oh, God, I wanted to cry and cry and never stop crying. Why didn't he just go and not say anything? I thought my teeth would smash and my jaw break in two from closing it so tightly. Nothing was said for a moment. Then the Brother started up the car.

I turned to the cop. 'Don't forget and tell me ma to write and come down and see me, please.'

'We must be on our way, say goodbye now,' the Brother said.

FOUR

We drove through the city of Galway and out into the countryside. The roads were narrow and twisting, mile after mile. We passed small villages, small shops and a huge forest of trees. People in fields and on the road waved at the car as it passed. The Brother waved back. After a while I began to wave back too. We didn't do much talking. He just asked what part of Dublin I came from, how many there was in the family, and if my mother and father were alive. I answered and said nothing else. I couldn't. It was strange being in a strange car with a Brother that you didn't know, going to a place that you didn't know either. All I had was thoughts that frightened me.

Looking through the windscreen, I could see huge mountains. They went up and up until you could see them no more, and, as the car moved, I would lose sight of them for a while. Then, on the next turn, they would appear again, kind of like magic and, as the car moved along the road, they became closer and closer until you could almost touch them.

Further on up the road we crossed a bridge. The Brother told me to look up at the side of this big mountain. 'Where will I look?' I asked, 'cause I couldn't see the top of it.

'There,' said the Brother, pointing his finger.

I could see this white statue of Jesus, and down from it there was a castle. The Brother stopped the car so I could get a better look. He knew what was going on in my mind, so he asked me how did that statue get up there. I looked at him.

'A crane brought it up,' I said.

'Think again, James,' said the Brother.

Maybe it's a miracle, I said to myself, too afraid to say it to the Brother.

'I don't know,' I said, 'it must have been always there.' He began to laugh to himself. I could see it. It made me feel uneasy, a dunce, I didn't let him see that though.

We passed along the road and I could see a road sign up ahead of us. I tried to figure out what it said, but I couldn't.

'Well, we're here. This is Letterfrack,' the Brother said.

As the car came into the small village, my heart began to pound with excitement and fear. I could see shops on the right and a pub. Before I had time to see anything else, the car turned to the left, up a small narrow road. Through the trees I could see a big white building. We turned to the right at the end of the road, coming through two gates which brought us into the school.

'Welcome to St Joseph's,' said Brother McCann.

The car came to a halt beside a row of small house-like buildings painted white with small windows. The Brother got out of the car and I followed. He put a hand on my shoulder and led me into the first of the small houses. As he pushed open the door, the top half of the door opened but the bottom half didn't. I watched him put his hand in through the half door. I could hear the bolt sliding back. He pushed the bottom half with his leg and in we went. Inside there was a counter, a few chairs, a stove fire and holy pictures hanging on the walls.

The floor was stone and there were boxes stacked against the walls. The only light in the room came through one small window. Brother McCann switched on a light, went behind the counter and began rooting around for something. There was a safe behind the counter and Brother McCann was trying to open it, but it seemed to be locked. He came out from behind the counter and told me to stay where I was, he'd be back in a moment. He went out the door and I stood stone still. Nothing was moving except my eyes and a clock that was sitting on a shelf behind the counter.

He returned shortly with an old Brother. The old Brother had a bunch of keys. He moved slowly in behind the counter and went over to the safe, opened it and took out a big heavy book and placed it on top of the counter and opened it. Brother McCann handed him the same papers that the policeman gave him in Galway. The old Brother took a pair of glasses from his pocket. Brother McCann asked me had I anything that I wanted him to mind for me, because it would be a lot safer in the safe. I gave him my matches, cigs and money and told him that that was all that I had. He put them on the table and counted the money. The old Brother was now writing what was on the papers into the big book. When he finished, he asked me had I any marks or was I ever sick or in hospital. I told him that I was in hospital once with a rash and another time when I got split open with a lump of coal. The old Brother didn't look at me once, he just kept on writing. Brother McCann told him to bring me to the tailor and the bootmaker's shop when he had finished with me. Brother McCann told me to be a good boy and left.

The old Brother stopped writing, closed the book, placed it back into the safe with my money and the papers that Brother McCann gave him, and locked the safe, all in a kind of slow motion. But he forgot me cigs. They were lying on the counter with the matches. He didn't put them into the safe. I thought that I was getting them back. I was sure of it, that the Brothers would let you smoke down here. I watched the old Brother slowly come out from behind the counter. He moved towards me, put a hand on my head. I thought he was going to fall or something. With his other hand he took the cigs and matches from the counter and, before I knew where they were, they were gone into his pocket. It must have been the fastest move the old bollix ever made.

He carefully locked up the office and then took me to the bootmaker's shop. The bootmaker asked me what size shoes I took. 'Size five I think.' He was standing behind a big table full of boots and shoes. He looked small and plumpish and an apron hung from his neck. I looked around the shop where some boys were working on shoes and others were polishing them. The bootmaker called to one of the boys who was working to get a pair of size five in a boot and a shoe. The boy did this and gave the shoes to the bootmaker. I stared at the other boys working, wondering to myself what this place was all about, but they soon caught me watching them and so I turned my eyes away. The bootmaker called me over to his side and told me to try on the shoes. Standing beside the bootmaker, I could see him in full. He seemed small alright but there was something about him. He didn't look like a Brother or a priest. I don't know why. He just didn't. I took the shoes from him, knelt down to untie my own shoes and take them off, and I got an awful fright. One of his legs was twisted and had a big boot on it. I could not take my eyes off it and I was terrified to look up at him. Quickly, I took off my own shoes and put on the new ones. They fitted me OK. The bootmaker asked were they hurting me.

'No, they fit,' I said.

'OK, you can take them off now and put back on your own.'

I did this quickly, 'cause I thought if I didn't, I might get clattered. The old Brother asked me was I ready. I said I was, trying hard not to look into the bootmaker's face. He might think that I was trying to be smart or that I was laughing at him. I walked over to the old Brother. 'Good luck now, Dinny,' he said as he opened the door.

I followed him out. I could see Dinny, the bootmaker, through the window of the shop and, as me and the Brother moved away to the tailor's shop, the bootmaker gave us a wave of his hand.

The tailor's shop was right next to the bootmaker's shop. About five boys sat up on a long table, sewing and talking to each other. I didn't look at these boys 'cause they were looking at me. First my eyes just took them in as we came into the shop. There was an older boy sitting beside a sewing machine. He stopped work to look me up and down. A big man stood near the window. I didn't know what he was doing but he stopped and came over to the old Brother and shook his hand. I thought to myself that he must be a brother of the bootmaker because he also had a big boot on his foot. Just then the fella on the sewing machine stood up to do something and he had a hump on his back. My head began to spin. 'Maybe that's what they do to you down here, make you go around with a hump on your back for not being good.'

The tailor measured me. I stood still as he measured the inside of my leg. When the tape touched me, I began to think he was one of those dirty men that give you sweets and run off with you and kill you. I could not really understand what they were supposed to do with you, but I had a feeling that it was something dirty and now this feeling was coming over me and neither me ma nor da was there to stop it. It wasn't that he was a dirty man. It was just that nobody had touched me there before and I knew it was kind of wrong or something.

It was over, and me and the Brother were out on the path again. 'Follow me,' he said and on we went down a flight of steps which led into a big yard, and in through a door on the left, and then in through another door which led into a shower-room. The room was cold and stony; water was dripping from some of the showers which were on both sides of the room. The Brother told me to wash myself. I began to take my clothes off and at the same time, tried to cover myself with them. Now and again I looked over at the Brother to see was he looking at me. I was praying that he would leave the room before I took off my pants but he stood there. I began to look around for a towel. There was none. Slowly, I sneaked off my trousers and held them in my hand to cover my privates. The Brother told me to get into the shower. I did. I stood in the shower looking around to find out how to turn on the water. My feet were cold from standing in the gully where the water went down the drain.

'Brother,' I called out, 'there's no water.'

He looked for a second, then went to the top of the shower, pulled a cord and out came the water and I washed and scrubbed. I got lost in the suds and the pouring water. The steam covered me up so no one could see me or me privates. I would have loved to stay in the water for ever, but the water stopped. There was a smell off the towel that the Brother gave me and when I had finished drying myself, I could smell the same smell off myself. The Brother told me to leave my own clothes where they were and come along. I wrapped the towel around myself and followed, wondering about my clothes and what was going to happen to them.

I came out of the shower-room and went along a corridor. There was a flight of stairs going up. I followed the old Brother who took years to get to the top. Once at the top, he opened a door to a huge dormitory with loads of beds all made up with white pillows and covered in blue, rows and rows of them. I stood inside and the Brother took a chart off the wall, looked at it and brought me down the side of the room to a bed with shoes and bundles of clothes on top of it. He told me to get dressed. I opened up the bundles. I found a vest and socks. Then I found a pair of underpants. I never wore underpants, only once, on me Communion day. I put them on. I thought I was sissy wearing these! Only girls wear them. They felt like knickers. Next was the trousers. I nearly dropped. The bleeding things were short trousers. I felt like roaring: 'I don't wear short fucking trousers. I want me long ones back.' I thought of the boys back in the flats laughing at me as I stood there wearing underpants and short trousers that made me look like a big fool.

I sat on the bed fiddling with my shoe, trying to understand what was happening to me. Everything that I owned was being taken away from me piece by piece, and was being replaced by something else and I couldn't fight it, or protect myself against it. There was nothing I could do about it except get used to it. The Brother was standing at the door of the dormitory. I jumped up off the bed and walked up to him. We both left the room and went down the same way we came up, past the shower-room and out into the big stone yard filled with sunshine, but I still felt a little cold, especially me legs.

FIVE

In the Industrial School you started your morning like everywhere else, by being woken up. Brother Michael would come in the morning and clap his hands and if your feet weren't on that floor by the third clap, God help you.

It was Halloween. My first four months had passed and I had got used to the place. To get used to a place like Letterfrack one has to change, and I felt that change come over me. Anyhow, if you weren't out of the bed you got thrown out by the Brother, mattress and all. It was always a good laugh until it happened to you. We used to wash ourselves in the washroom just outside the dormo and you couldn't go out there wearing the top of your pyjamas. Brother Michael never thought it was too cold. After washing and making your bed, every bed made the same way, you got into line with the clap of the Brother's hands, and went down the stairs and into the yard and stood there until the older boys got down from St Joseph's dormo. Our dormo, St Michael's, was for younger boys from seven to eleven.

When everybody was in the yard, we climbed up a steep set of steps to the chapel. It was so dark in the morning, you could hardly see where you were walking and sometimes the steps would be like ice and you would slip and smack your face off the freezing cold stone. But once you were inside the church, you got warmer with the four walls and all the bodies to keep the cold away. After Mass we all went back down to the yard and played for a while until the bell was rung for breakfast. Every boy would move as fast as he could to get to the top of his line which was painted on the ground in the yard. Every table had eight boys, four at each end of the table. If you got to the top of your line before anyone else, you'd be able to get to the table first. All you had to do then was touch all the food on the table with your hand and say it was yours. Anything you touched first was yours and the rest of the table had to offer you something for it in return.

After breakfast, the washing-up was done by whosever turn it was to do it. It was always done by two boys, one washing and the other drying. After breakfast everybody, except the boys that had to wash up, went back out into the yard to play for a while. The legs would be frozed off you because of the short trousers. Everyone wore shorts. Only the boys that worked on the farmyard could wear long ones. They had to get up much earlier than us to milk the cows and clean out the farmyard. It was getting brighter as we played around the yard. Everything stopped as the Brothers clapped their hands for us to line up for school.

There were about five classrooms on the ground floor, just in off the yard under St Joseph's dormo. The classes were the same as anywhere else, the pupils ranging from those who knew nothing to those who knew everything. My class was a kind of half-dunce class and Brother Michael was our teacher and the biggest bastard that ever was. He had dark hair and a pointy nose and told us he was thirty-three. Our classroom was full of rocks, bits of trees, jars full of muck, and books. In the morning we would go to our classroom, led by Brother Michael, and begin our morning prayer. We got soup and bread at eleven o'clock, then back to school till two o'clock.

After school we would all go back into the yard and line up according to where you worked. The work places were the farm, where most of the lads worked, the bootmaker's shop, the tailor's shop, the cleaner's and the kitchen. I worked in the laundry, washing clothes. Another lad called Behan worked with me. In the summer it was poxy cause the bollix would be burnt off you with the heat of the place, but now that it was cold it was a good job 'cause of all the hot water and all the nice warm steam. The worst places to work in the winter were the fields and the bog, crying with the pain of the cold. After an hour, numb and working like a machine, you couldn't even cry any more.

From half-two to half-six you did your day's work, no matter what the weather was. Then stop for your tea, line up, into the dining-hall, stand quietly for all to enter. Brother Duncan would stand at the top of the hall under the holy picture, watching the boys, making sure that they did not behave like animals or savages. Everyone in, prayers, sit down and bargain. If one got the tea, he could swap it for bread or egg or whatever. The bread was always green-mouldy. Even when you brought it up to the Brother and got a new one, it was the same and when you told the Brother this, he told you to cut off the bad bits and eat the good bits, but you got used to the food being the way it was and that was that. After tea, the same as after breakfast and dinner, two boys washed up and any boy who was to get beaten stood against the wall. Brother Duncan had a rubber strap that he had made in the bootmaker's shop. He always hit you on the wrist and always looked as if he was biting his tongue.

If it rained after tea we would all go into the rec. hall. It had a stage and a big wooden floor. There was a TV in the corner near the stage, table-tennis in the middle of the floor, or you could make up your own games. At the other end of the hall, there was a small room in which the Brothers showed films. The Brothers sat at different places around the hall. After tea, this was where we played. There was a big stove fire in the hall and a lot of the lads would sit around it, not so much to get a heat as to have a smoke, mostly butts picked up off the ground. But when things were bad it was bootlaces or turf mould rolled up in jax paper. It wasn't a bad smoke and it made you feel a little bit bigger or harder or whatever. You'd finish up in the hall about eight or half-eight and go up to your dormo, undress, wash face, neck and hands and feet, say your prayers, swap comics or anything that you had. The radio would be turned on for a while. Sometimes the Beatles would be playing. I liked them, we all did. I'd say the Brothers did too. Before you went to sleep you had to go to the toilet. If you were a piss-in-the-bed, then you would have to tie a sheet to the end of your bed for the night watchman to wake you up and get you to go to the toilet.

When the lights went out, Brother Michael would go to his room. His room had a little window so he could look in at the dormo in case there might be a fight or something. I would put my head under the bedclothes to get myself nice and cosy. I could hear the rain bashing against the windows and the sound of the wind charging through the school building, making a whistling noise. I would just lie there thinking of me ma and about going home.

Me best pal that I hung around with was Eamon Doyle. He was going home soon. Before I got sent to Letterfrack, me and Eamon used to go on the hop from school and go off robbin' together. We used to really enjoy ourselves. His ma was always tellin' him to keep away from me and my ma used to tell me the same. One day after school I went home to the flats to meet Eamon Doyle, to go off together. When I got into the flats me ma was standing outside the hall door looking for one of my sisters to mind my younger brother Thomas. There was none of them to be found and, seeing me, she called me to come to the flat and take Thomas out and mind him till teatime. I didn't want to mind him. You couldn't climb or scut lorries with a baby. Anyhow he was always bleeding crying. I told me ma that I didn't want to mind him and that I was always stuck with him. Ma told me to come up and take him out or she'd tell me da when he came home from work. I brought my brother down into the yard in the flats to play, all the time keeping my eye on Doyle's hall door, waiting for Eamon to come out. I could hear his hobnail boots sliding along the landing and running down the stairs. They were great boots, made of leather and they had lots of studs on them. Doyle asked me was I going off up the Naller.

'Yeah,' I said, 'but we're going to have to sneak out of the flats and not let my brother Thomas see us 'cause he'll follow us.'

Soon we were over by Jacob's factory, running really fast 'cause me brother was bound to follow us. We got to Bride Street and we were dashing across the road. Eamon was in front of me and I could see a Mini car coming towards him. I told him to look out and he tried to stop but his hobnail boots slid all over the place. The car hit him a bang, and he was taken off in an ambulance to hospital. I had to go back to the flats and tell his ma. I just told her that he slipped on his hobnail boots and got a smack of a car but that he was alright. Eamon was sent from Artane Industrial School to Letterfrack over getting into fights. We shared things, sweets and parcels that were sent from home, and, if I was fighting somebody and anybody jumped in, then Eamon would jump in for me.

The Brothers brought all the boys on a three-mile walk to Kylemore Abbey every Sunday. All of us would be in our Sunday suits and shoes. We all walked in twos out of the school gates, into the village and off we went. Me and Doyle walked together, and always tried to get as near to the top of the line as we could because people in cars would throw their cig ends out of their cars and they would be laying along the roadside and, if you were at the bottom of the line, you never got a tap, because loads of pairs of eyes and hands were there before you. The tourists would take pictures of us walking along the road. I used to think that they thought that we were orphans or something. They never talked to us, only to the Brothers. The Americans loved it and would give us dollars to buy sweets, but the Brothers always watched us and when we got back to the school, we would have to hand it up. Every boy loved the walk. It was good to get out and you never knew what you might find on the road.

When Eamon Doyle finished his sentence I was very sad for a while, but I got over it. Anyway, I had made friends with others and I knew what most boys had been sent down here for and knew all their names. I never hung around with anybody in particular. I was mainly on my own. I used to miss me ma and da a lot and loved it when I got a letter from home. Brother 'Shock' was in charge of handing out the letters and the parcels that came in for us. We called him Shock because he nearly electrocuted himself fixing a light in the hall one night. He would come into the playing yard at lunch-break with a bunch of letters in his hand. Sometimes he would call out the names and everybody would be waiting to hear theirs being called. Other times he would walk about the yard with his hands in his pockets and every few minutes he would nod to some boy and the boy would go running up to him.

When he called me I couldn't move quick enough. I was always a bit too quick in asking for my letter, so he would hold on to it for a while just for a laugh. He would say things like, 'Do you know anybody from Dublin?' or, 'Would you like to have a letter from home?' After taunting me for a while, he'd give me my letter, which was always already opened and read. Also my ma used to send me down money to buy things and Shock would take this money out and write on the front of the envelope how much was in the letter. Then he'd give me the letter but I'd have to hand it back to him to read out because I couldn't read it myself.

My mother would write all about home, how Eamon Doyle was getting on, how much she missed me and all the family missed me, but that I was not to worry, as it wouldn't be long now till we saw each other again and that God was good and he would mind me.

I still didn't like school, but in St Joseph's I had to go to class. There was about ten blokes in our class. Brother Michael would bring the whole class up the mountain to collect rocks and weeds and all sorts of other things, and you had to carry all these rocks and muck and sometimes even stingers all the way back down the mountain and into the class.

The weather got bitterly cold. I used to hate getting out of bed in the cold early morning. Not only that, but you had to wash your neck even if it was not dirty. But the real thing that I hated was the bog and the farm and the miles and miles of fields. One freezing day, when Mrs Kelly, the woman who worked in the laundry, didn't come in to work me and Behan were told to get rubber boots on and go to work in the fields.

There was a big line of boys coming out of the storeroom with boots too big for them, boots too small, boots with holes in them, fellas coming into the yard with boots that were odd boots, that were on the wrong foot and, as they came out, those that were going in slagged and jeered them. I went to the bottom of the queue in the hope that when I got into the storeroom there would be no boots left, and I wouldn't have to go out into the fields. But no, and soon I was standing in the middle of a huge bog filling bags with ice-cold turf. After about half an hour of this you either became like a machine or you cracked up from the cold. You just had to keep going to keep the heat that was in your body alive. All we had to wear was a short coat, a jumper, vest, underpants, our short pants and a pair of wellies.

Everybody was working away in pairs. One held the bag, while the other loaded it up. When the bags were full of turf, you had to carry them on your back up to the tractor and trailer to Johnny Lamb, the farm worker. He'd make sure that no boy was bringing half-empty bags. Some of us often did this because they were too heavy for us. If you got caught, he would clatter you about the ears until your whole face was bright red and roasting hot. Then you would be put working where he could see you and you would never get a minute's peace.

We worked into the afternoon before we got our break. Some of the boys got into groups and chatted and the boys at the other end of the bog messed, throwing bits of turf at each other. The lads that I stood with looked as if they had all been crying as their eyes were filled with water from the sharp wind that sliced down from the hills and mountains that surrounded us. Tony Keane always carried a pack of cards with him. He was a tough Crumlin bloke who loved playing knuckles and it wasn't long before he had the group of us playing with him. We all won a few hands each, all was quite soft and easy, mainly because no one had the strength to put any force behind the blows, but it was a different story when Tony Keane won a good round. He was ready to give everybody twelve knuckles and he was going for blood. Everybody started to blow their hot breath into their hands to get life back into them. Getting a wallop of a pack of cards on your cold hands stings something brutal.

He knew that he had us all by the bollix when he told us that we could swap our knuckles for the scrambled eggs that we were getting for our tea. With the thought of my scrambled eggs going into the mouth of Tony Keane and nothing but fresh air going into mine, I put out my hands. It was not until the sting from the blow ran through me that it dawned on me that that hand out there in front of him was part of me. I was nearly going to offer him half my scrambled eggs to stop and call it quits. It seemed like a long time since the first wallop, but now I was sitting down on a mound of turf holding my arms under my armpits to try and ease the pain and stinging. My mind was taken off the pain when I watched the rest get their knuckles. I started to laugh as they jumped and hopped about, pulling their knuckles away. Joey Finn told me to shut up or I would get my head kicked off so I shut up. Tony Keane finished giving out the last of the knuckles. Then he put his cards back into his pocket and walked off grinning through his hare-lip.

Soon we were all told to get back to work. We worked until it was nearly dark, pulling up turf out of the bog, filling up the bags, putting the bags up on our backs to bring up to the tractor to be brought off and burnt to keep some bollix warm. We were on our way now down the long twisting bog road, all of us more or less in a straight line. I was starving. All

I could think of was the big pot of tea, millions of slices of bread and tons of scrambled eggs. I was always hungry, always thinking of food. The tractor which was at the front of the line leading us down the path began to take up speed and so did I and all the rest of the boys. We even passed out the tractor and the run turned into a race to see who would be the first to reach the school. By the time everybody had put their boots into the store and then washed themselves, it was nearly half-past six, time for our tea.

We were all walking or playing in the yard, waiting for the dining-hall bell to go. Some boys were even standing on their table line. The door of the dining-hall opened and before the bell was even heard, there was a stampede to get into line. Brother Moy and Brother Byrne stood in front of the line. We all stood waiting for them to tell us to move and they never did this until there was total silence and everybody was standing still. Then Brother Moy gave his hand signal and the first line moved quietly, almost on air, up the three steps and into the huge dining-hall. Line after line after line, then my line, then more lines until all were present and standing, each at their table. No boy was allowed eat or touch anything on the table until the Brother gave his signal, but he couldn't see all the boys at once, and those who were quick could touch any food on the table. Most times everybody would get a chance to touch something and you could bargain. The boys on my table weren't bad. At some of the other tables all you'd get would be the leftovers or the slop.

In the name of the Father and of the Son, and of the Holy Ghost, Amen. We give Thee thanks Lord for all Thy bounty which we are about to receive, through Christ Our Lord, Amen. Cups on saucers, spoons stirring in cups, chairs scraping upon the floor, voices talking, mouths eating, bellies filling, plates falling, smashing, faces smiling, teapots boiling, knives and forks rattling on shining delph, and the white bread is green-mouldy, but I am far too hungry so I will eat it up; the scrambled egg is mangled, mingled with the green mould, sciddering down my throat. Me and seven at the table eating like horses in a stable, food munched, tea drained. In the name of the Father and of the Son and of the Holy Ghost, Amen. We give Thee thanks for our food O Lord. It was now pitch-black in the sky outside the window as we all left the dining-hall, table after table, then mine, then more.

Me ma wrote more and more letters to me, and as time passed I was getting to be able to read them on my own, but when I was writing back I still had to get Brother Sparks to do the spelling for me. I kept all my letters in the pillowcase on my bed; that was the safest place and the warmest place and that's where I was now, half-thinking, half-dreaming about home, my family and Ma. Everybody seemed to be asleep. Somebody was muttering in his sleep but I couldn't make out where it was coming from. I sat up in my bed to have a look, but all went quiet again. My eyes moved around the dormo. Tony Keane had himself wrapped up like a mummy in his blanket. There was some beds empty, boys used to fall out from moving about in their sleep. I could hear footsteps coming from St Joseph's where the bigger boys slept. The sound was moving towards our dormo. I slid down into my bed.

The light in the jax was switched on. Standing at the door of the dormo was Mr Keeler, the watchman. In his hand were the keys and a flashlamp. Switching on his flashlamp, he moved into the dormo. Any bed that had a sheet tied to the end of the bed meant that the boy who slept there was a piss-in-the-bed, and the watchman would have to come every few hours to wake up the piss-in-the-beds to get them to go to the jax. There were about ten sailors in our dormo and Mr Keeler went about the dormo waking them all up with his flashlamp. I watched him move about the room, shaking the boys awake. Those who didn't wake up, he ripped the bedcovers off them and shoved his flashlamp into their faces.

Scabby-faced Fitzgerald was the last boy that the watchman went to wake up. All the rest of the sailors were back in their beds now, only Fitzgerald was left. Nobody in the school liked Fitzgerald because he had scabs around his mouth and everybody said that he got them from gobbling the watchman. Some of the blokes would not even look at Fitzgerald, and if he walked into a group of boys and there was no Brother about, the boys would kick and punch him, spit at him and call him a scabby-faced gobbler.

Now the watchman was standing beside Fitzgerald's bed. I held my breath and didn't dare move for fear of being caught. The watchman switched off his lamp. I watched him put his hand under Fitzgerald's bedclothes. My mouth was dry, my whole body felt wet and the sheets felt as if they were sticking to me. I got frightened and didn't want to watch anymore. I pulled the blankets over my head. My heart was pounding so loudly in my chest that I thought the watchman had heard it and was coming towards me. I could hear the footsteps getting closer and closer while I prayed for sleep, closing my eyes tighter and tighter until there was pain. The footsteps passed me, no sound. Everything quiet. Then the sound of the jax light being switched off, then sleep.

Deep sleep, twisting and twitching, darkness. I can see the darkness when my eyes open and when my eyes close, alone, nothing to touch, no one to touch me. Emptiness. Nothingness. The sea down below. Waves bashing against the rocks. Fear, must get back. Fight the wind. Don't let it take me.

Don't let it push me to leave me smashed open on the rocks. Hold on to the grass, the hair of the earth's head. Come away from there Ma, you'll fall. Mammy, Mammy please. I'm sorry, Ma. She can't hear me. I can only watch her crying. She's going to fall. I can't stop her. No, not me, Ma. Please not me, Ma. Gone, she's gone. And I can't reach her. Her eyes open but gone forever. The thundering of the waves, water in my eyes, blanket, sheet, pillow, bed, dormo, awake, awake. Calm now, only a dream. Ma's at home. Must get home. I love you Ma … asleep.

SIX

At home sometimes I slept in the top bunk in the front bedroom, sometimes in the pram shed. One night me ma went out
with my Uncle Francis, who had just come home from Eng-
land. I was hiding on the stairs in the flats with Lassie, a big
sheepdog I had found running around the streets that day.
The both of us watched as me ma and me uncle went down
the other stairs and out the gate, heading for the pub. When
they had gone, I brought Lassie up the stairs and sneaked him
into the back bedroom of the flat and told him to stay there. I
closed the bedroom door over and went into the front room.

'Where were you all day, you little bastard?' said Martina.
I didn't say anything. 'Did you go to school today?' I nodded.
'You're a fucking liar. You were seen with Eamon Doyle rob-
bing down in Grafton Street.'

'That wasn't me,' I said.

'You just wait till me ma gets back,' Martina said back to
me, with half a laugh.

If I had not got Lassie hiding in the back bedroom, I would
have told Martina that she was a gunner-eyed swine and that,
if she told Ma about me and got me a beating, then I would tell
Ma about her being with fellas, and buyin' sweets and then,

when me ma was finished hitting me, she would reef Martina around the house for filling her big mouth with the sweets bought out of me ma's money. But I didn't say a word. I just let her laugh at the thoughts of me getting a beating from me ma. I was now trying to think of a way to sneak some food out of the press and then sneak myself and Lassie out of the flat.

Martina sat down by the fire, her gunner-eyes were glued to the TV. I went into the scullery and opened the cupboard. I could see a lump of meat on the bottom shelf. I had a look to see was I being watched. Martina was still looking at the TV. I could see her jaws moving up and down, and hear the noise of the sweets being crushed in her mouth. Before I had time to think, my hand had moved and the meat was under me jumper. I put the cup back into the press, and moved the lump of meat up me jumper and held it under my arm 'cause that way it does not show so much. I came out of the kitchen. Martina was still looking at the TV.

'I'm going to the toilet,' I said, feeling nervous.

'Go where you like,' Martina snapped back. 'You're still going to get it when me ma comes back.'

I went into the hall and opened the back bedroom door, coughing and whistling so she wouldn't hear. Just then the dog started to bark. Fuck, now I had to move fast. I made a go for the hall door. I had just about got through when Martina appeared at the other door, the dark hallway lit up from the light coming from the sitting-room. My head darted from side to side, looking for me dog. No sign of him anywhere. I gave a short whistle. 'Here Lassie, come on boy.'

'Oh, you just wait, James O'Neill, you're going to get it. Where's that dog?'

'Fuck off, gunner-eye. He's in the bedroom and if you go near me, he'll eat you,' I said, trying to frighten her and also remembering the beating she got me a few days ago.

'Get that dog out of the flat, you humpy swine.'

The dog was now between the two of us, wondering which way to go and who to go to. Feeling a bit braver with the dog there, I moved into the hall to get him.

'Go on,' I said to Martina. 'Slag me now, go on, say something and I'll get Lassie to eat the hands off you.'

Taking my eyes off Martina, I bent down to get hold of the rope that I had around the dog's neck and as I got the rope into my hand, Martina flung a Toffolux sweet. It hit me right in the face and it hurt. I jumped to my feet and made a go for Martina. I was too far away from her and, before I could reach her, she ran into the sitting-room, slammed the door and held her back against it to stop me getting at her. I kicked the door in temper, crying in rage, but she just laughed, and said: 'You just wait, you just wait.'

I left the house with Lassie and the meat under my arm, slamming the hall door behind me and nearly breaking the glass that was already cracked. I ran down the stairs, the dog by my side. When I got down into the flats, Martina was standing on the balcony with a pot of water, daring me and slagging me. But I knew that she was only trying to get me to come forward and that she would drown me with the water. I shouted up to her.

'I can see the water, you big pig. You should wash your gee with it.' It was only when it was out that I realized what I had said, and I knew that after saying that, I couldn't go home 'cause I'd get a battering and be sent to bed. Martina would make sure of that. I looked up. I could see her standing on the balcony, the light still shining from the sitting-room through the hall and hitting her in the back. I laughed and taunted her till I got her raging. Her arm moved up as if I was in front of her and she was going to hit me with the pot. The pot left her hand and went tumbling into the air. The water left the pot. I could see it come rushing towards me like a net trying to catch me. But me and Lassie were well away from even getting a drop. The water hit the ground first and splashed everywhere. The pot hit the ground, its handle smashing to bits. 'You just wait, you just wait,' I could hear her scream as we left the flats, going nowhere, with nowhere in mind.

We ran along Mercer Street, up to Cuffe Street, going faster and faster, till we reached Montague Lane, then out into the light of Montague Street until it felt safe. We walked up along the canal and sat on the grass, flung stones into the water and me and Lassie ate the meat. Then we walked the length of the Naller until it was quiet and there were few cars passing and nobody in sight. I thought of me warm bed, but I knew I couldn't go back. Even if I wanted to get into the house, I was sure gunner-eye would have locked up the windows to stop me from climbing in. But I knew that she couldn't lock the pram shed 'cause the lock was always broken. There wasn't a soul about the streets as we trotted back to the flats to sleep in the pram shed. The only noise was the odd car passing and the sound of paper being blown around the street by the wind.

All the flats were in darkness, only the street lamp that hung on the side wall of the flats was lit. The pram shed was empty except for some fruit boxes, a few bags of cabbage and a few old coats that me ma wore when she went out to sell fruit. I got Lassie in and closed the door, put the coats on the ground, then me and the dog lay down beside each other. I asked God not to let anybody take Lassie away, then I went off to sleep.

Brother Michael clapped his hands and I jumped out from my bed. All about me the rest of the lads were hopping onto the floor and grabbing their towels and heading for the wash-hand basins, every one of them stripped to the waist. It was always best to try and get to the washroom first, otherwise you had to wait in line until someone had finished and that meant standing in the cold in the bottoms of your pyjamas. I got a sink. I washed my face, neck and ears and hands, brushed my teeth and went back into the dormo to make up my bed and dress myself. Boys waited in line to use the washroom, watched over by Brother Michael.

'Get in there boy and scrub that filthy neck of yours,' he screamed at one of the lads, 'before I get out the hose.'

Macker Burke was a headcase, he was always talking about girls, knickers, diddies, bras and gees. One day in class, Brother Michael let us all see a film about the jungle. Half-way through the film, a big black woman's diddies came on the screen. When I saw them, I got flashes of Mrs Kelly's diddies in my mind. I used to wonder what was under her jumper and how nice they looked from the corner of my eye, but I could never understand what you were supposed to do with them or what they were even for. Now, a big pair of black diddies were right in front of my eyes and I could see Mrs Kelly's and imagine her holding me, and a strange feeling came over me, ran through me. I couldn't see her face, only her diddies, and I didn't know what to do. Then Macker Burke kicked the back of my chair. 'Get up there, Neiller, and suck them,' he said.

Before I could get up off the ground, Brother Michael was on top of Macker, clattering him, punching him.

'What did I hear you say? What did I hear you say?'

'I didn't say anything, I swear, Brother. It wasn't me,' Macker said, terrified.

'Stand there against that wall until I'm ready for you.'

I was now standing on my feet. Brother Michael switched on the light, told two boys to roll up the blinds.

'There will be no more films ever,' he said and in the same breath, 'O'Neill, join Burke. The rest of you boys out into the yard.'

The classroom door closed. I could hear the key being turned in the lock but dared not turn and look. The Brother sat up on one of the desks and called Burke over to him.

'Now, what did you say?'

'Nothing,' said Burke.

'Right, we will see what sounds an animal like yourself can make with that filthy tongue of yours.'

The drumstick came whistling through the air over and over again. Sometimes the Brother would lash the stick down on Macker's hand and at the same time wallop him across the face and ears with his other hand. Macker was screaming for mercy, saying that he was sorry. When the Brother was finished, he grabbed Macker's hair, pulled him onto his tippy-toes, kicked him to the door and booted him to the ground outside the classroom. The door slammed shut. I was trembling. As the Brother faced the door for a moment and then turned to me, I could feel my whole stomach heave to my mouth. Tears were filling my eyes.

'Stop that crying, O'Neill. I haven't even started on Burke yet.'

I stopped quickly by holding my breath.

'Now,' said the Brother, 'are you going to tell me what Burke said, and why he pushed you onto the floor?'

'I don't know, Brother,' I said. He took me by my lip, pulled me up to the front of the classroom.

'Now,' he said, 'I was not going to slap you if you told me the truth, but you chose to tell me more lies. Take down your pants.'

My blood raced all round my body. I got terrified, screamed

that I would tell the truth. 'Oh please, I'm sorry, I won't do it again. I'll be good.'

'Shut your mouth, you're getting what you asked for.'

I was in complete hysteria. He dragged me over the desk by the hair, lashed my hands away from me holding onto my pants, and pulled them down. Everything was running through my mind at once, the film, the poxy film. Macker Burke started this, the bastard. He should never had said what he said. I lay there waiting for the first lash, my heartbeat getting faster and faster, and the images of the big black diddies, big diddies, Mrs Kelly's diddies; I lay there not knowing what to do, looking at them. What did Macker say? What did he say? Suck them, Neiller … suck, lash, suck, lash, suck, lash, suck, lash. Now I could see what they were for, the picture clear as the film but it is a sin, wrong, bad, go away, get out of my mind, tears, crying sorry, sore, sore.

'Now, O'Neill. You won't be falling off chairs anymore! Well, not for a while anyhow. Get out where you belong, into the jungle with the rest of the monkeys, before I change my mind and cut the skin off you.'

I opened the classroom door slowly, walked down the corridor and into the yard. A gang of boys surrounded Macker Burke. He came over to me, the gang following hot on his heels. Now they all surrounded me. I moved closer to the wall. 'How many did he give you?' Macker asked, then everybody asked, 'How many?', 'How many?' My hand moved to my face in time to catch the tears, the snot and the dribble. I held my hands to my face until they all left, until the bell rang for dinner, and, like the rest of the boys, I sprang into line.

For days my arse was very sore, and when I was at class, I kept well away from Macker Burke and out of trouble. I knew Brother Michael was only waiting for a chance to lash me again. I was going to be a good boy and not look at or even think about Mrs Kelly's diddies again, and I asked God to help me every night before I went to sleep. But it was no good. I could never keep out of trouble nor keep the sight of the diddies from my mind.

At work I watched Mrs Kelly putting clothes in the washer, stooping down to the ground and lifting handfuls of shirts and pants and letting them fall from her hands into the washer which was like a big round drum, pile after pile, until it was full. Then she closed the steel door tightly and stood back from it, her eyes searching for something. She moved towards a small wooden table. There were twenty Sweet Afton and a box of matches lying on it. She picked up her smokes, lit one and then walked back to the washer, pushed the start button and began the wash.

Rows of nice neatly ironed shirts sat to one side of my table, on the other side piles of crumpled ones. The hot iron was in my right hand, and with my left, I took a shirt from the pile. The iron pressed down onto the shirt, slid right up to the collar. In a few seconds the shirt that was crumpled and creased sat neatly on top of the pile like a brand new shirt, unspoiled by sweat or dirt. Patrick Behan was inside the drying room, placing the wet clothes on the huge dry horses. The whole laundry was in full swing, spinners, washers, dryers all in motion, out to kill the dirt with such devotion, dirty sheets, stinking socks, all piled up in stacks, while nice clean shirts, smoothly pressed, lie sleeping in small packs. Rumble, tumble, rumble, spinning all around. Out comes the black-grey water splashing on the ground.

Mrs Kelly finished her smoke and pushed the button to stop the washer. I watched her unload the wet clothes into the spinner. She had to bend over the washer and reach into it.

71

Each time she bent over, my eyes would watch her and, each time she turned to carry the clothes over to the spinner, my eyes would dart back onto my work and my face would get red and my body would grow warm all over with an excitement that I tried to but could not understand.

I watched her legs, her face, watched her all over. As she moved across the floor to get the last of the wet clothes from the washer, I watched her move her head right into the washer to see if any clothes were left at the bottom of the machine. She moved her whole body in a bending motion straight into the machine. Her legs lifted off the ground. My heart moved and caught in the middle of my throat. My eyes locked. My body went numb. Her skirt had lifted straight up her legs. I could see everything, her knickers, the top of her legs, her bum. I could almost touch them. Everything went still in my mind. I heard no sound, felt no pain, needed no air. I couldn't take my eyes off her. Suddenly she was looking at me. I felt my face burn as hot as the iron in my hand, felt myself sinking down, wanting to crawl away, never to return.

Mrs Kelly had her hair brushed back over her head and it came out around her neck in light-brown curls. She smiled to herself as if she knew my secret. Our eyes broke off and she moved away. I felt like a child, like a real baby caught playing with himself by his mammy. I wanted to die there and then. But I didn't. I noticed Patrick Behan staring right into my face and I darted back to my work, wondering whether he had seen what I had seen and did he feel the same. But there was one thing I was sure of, I was not going to ask him 'cause he might think I was being dirty or something. I worked and worked, as hard as I could, feeling awkward and self-conscious and trying to hide my feelings and destroy the picture that was now planted in my mind.

I told Mrs Kelly that I was going to the toilet. I walked through the corridors that ran along beside the shower-room and out across the playing-yard which was empty and lifeless, and into the row of cubicles. There wasn't a soul about as I sat in the cubicle and even if somebody did come, I'd be able to see them over the half-door of the toilet. They were that way so the Brothers could keep an eye on what was going on.

I took my pants down and looked at my birdy. There were little hairs. I could just barely see them, I could just barely feel them, soft, all soft, everything soft and nice and nobody to hide from, no one about. Alone. I could see her, could see up her clothes, feel her, touch her, look into her face and not be afeared that she would tell the Brothers on me. We were alone. My hand was her hand now, touching me, rubbing me up and down, soft and gentle, then hard and strong. My legs stiffened. My birdy got hard and big. Everything started to rush all around inside me, getting faster and faster, lifting me somewhere, watching her skirt lift up and up, looking at me. Breathing, can't breathe. Ah, must get air. Faster, faster, faster, spinning round and round. Stiff, hard, soft, rub, rubbing, holding tighter and tighter, squeezing, hot, cold, burning, roasting fire. Can't get out, don't want to get out Ahhhhhhh-hhhhhhhhhhh. Exploding inside, bursting out blood, red and silky soft, red, then white on my hands, on the ground, dropping slowly down the wall, breathing deeply, quickly. Gulps in, fresh, cold, watching hot come pouring out into the air. Stinging pain, feeling it breathe in my hand, big, pump, pump, hard then soft, softer, smaller.

Blood, fright, look around. Where am I? Who's there? How long have I been here? What happened, quick, hurry, rush, panic, run, fast, laundry door, hold it. Stop. Wait …

I opened the door and almost got a fright from all the noise

SEVEN

James O'Neill
St Joseph's Industrial School
Letterfrack
Co Galway

Dear Ma and Da and family,

Just a line to let you know how I am getting on. I am getting on fine. I hope you are fine too. The weather down here is freezing and snowing but you get used to it after a while. Ma, I am not going home for Christmas holidays but I might be home for summer holidays, because I got into trouble a few times and anyhow the Brother told me you have to be a year and a month down here before you can go home on holiday. Will you come down and visit me? How is all the family? Is Eamon Doyle working? Tommy Byrne our cousin is down here and so is Ed Newman. I know nearly everybody down here. When I get out I am going to get a job. I won't get into trouble again. I miss you and all the family and the flats but maybe I will get off on my appeal and then I won't have to come back down here. I got your last letter and the money that you sent me and the food parcel. Sometimes I share the things

I get with Tommy Byrne, that is all I can say for now until I get a letter from you and will you send me some money for Christmas and tell everybody that I was asking for them.

I love you Ma and Da and all the family.

Write soon. I miss you all, love James

P.S. HAPPY XMAS AND MERRY NEW YEAR

All those that got their signed forms back from home had big smiling happy faces. The school was full of excitement. Only a few days more and they would be off home, some for good, some just for the Christmas holidays. Me and the other boys who weren't going home couldn't understand why some boys that had only been in the kip a few months were getting to go home for Christmas. Sometimes I sobbed on my own, thinking about being home for Christmas, but there was no use crying. I was not going home and that was that.

'Ah sure, you'll be after having a grand time here for Christmas, cake, pudding, the lot. Sure you might not get that at home. Aren't you well off here? Don't mind those that are going home,' said Brother Lennon, who I hated 'cause he was always running his fingers through my hair. I felt that he was making a joke out of me, the same way that he was always making a joke out of Mickey Mitchell, who was sitting beside him now with a lake of snot running down his nose, his lower lip on top of his upper lip making sure that he didn't miss a drop. Now and again he would cease work, draining his canal of snot, and look up at me with his gunner-eyes. Then he would get back to work, first shoving half his finger up his nose, then the tongue would come out of his mouth and lick his upper lip. Boys used to give him things to let them see him put his tongue up his nose. He was the only one in the whole school who could do that.

Brother Lennon kept on at me. I wasn't listening to him. I was nearly getting sick on top of the two of them. I don't know how I held it in. Brother Lennon told me to go and play and I was gone like a flash.

The hall was real noisy, everybody bubbling, everybody friendly to each other, but I knew that it was only because of the holidays. Joey Finn, Tony Keane and Ballyer were huddled around the turf fire at the top of the hall. They too were staying for Christmas but they looked as if they didn't give a bollix. I sat down beside them.

'Licking the Brother's arse for Christmas holidays, were you Neiller?' 'No,' says Joey Finn. 'He was gobbling him.'

My temper started to go 'cause I knew that Finn was only acting hard 'cause he was with Tony Keane. Any time he was with Keaner, he slagged everybody that Tony Keane could do in a fight, because he knew that, if he got claimed, Tony Keane would go in for him. So he kept slagging me and the others laughed: 'I wouldn't let anybody away with slagging me like that.' 'Stick it on him Neiller.' 'That fucking fool couldn't stick a stamp on a letter.' 'He's a bleeding idiot.'

I exploded. I came down on Finn like a wild savage. I wanted to smash him to pieces. I didn't even think about Tony Keane. I'd lost my temper. We smashed to the floor. His head hit me in the face and his hand gripped tightly onto my hair while he kicked and punched me. I couldn't do anything, I was in too much of a temper and he was battering me. To stop getting the punches in the face, I held myself close to him on the floor hoping that the Brothers would come soon and stop the fight. I could feel the hall go quiet except for the TV. A lot of boys were gathered around us. 'Neiller, you're a poxy goer.'

'Go on, Joey, give it to him.' 'He started it,' I could hear them slag me. Joey Finn was beating me, I didn't fight back hoping that he would stop.

'Oh please, somebody stop him from hitting me. I'm sorry Joey, you can do me,' but he wouldn't listen. I screamed and struggled. I could feel lumps of my hair coming out, kicks at my legs, smacks from his fist. Somebody spitting at me. Hurt, pain, blood, tears. Only one way, trapped, open mouth, wool, linen, cotton, flesh, blood, scream, free, free. Everybody looking at me. 'Here's the Brother,' somebody shouted.

I looked down at Joey Finn, roaring in pain on the floor, blood all over his clothes and beside him a piece of his chest. Brother Lennon's hand came thundering across my face and lifted me off the ground. On my way up from the floor, I caught hold of the turf bucket and let it fly, then I made a dash towards the door of the recreation hall.

I didn't know where I was going, fear was charging through me, my heart pounding in my chest, and my legs carrying me at full speed into the darkness. Through fields, over bogs, up and down slippy hills, onto roads, into bushes, plunging through the wind and rain, under the stars in the light of the moon, soaking wet from head to toe, hot with sweat, on, on I gotta go. I hid by the main road in a watery ditch. I could hear the cars pass, watch their lights light up the road as they passed. Then darkness and quiet would creep back into place, still, resting until the next car. I didn't know where I was. How far was I from the school? How long had I been running? Could I make it to Dublin? They would all be out trying to catch me – farmers, Brothers, police. Nobody has ever escaped from here. Must not go onto the road. The fear sent shivers throughout my whole body at the thoughts of what the Brothers would do to me when they caught me. And then I would have to face Joey Finn and Keaner. Fuck it. He started it. I am glad that I bit him.

The rain trickled down from my hair and dropped onto my face. My feet were getting very cold. I rubbed my legs to keep them warm. I thought that the best thing to do would be to find a barn and sleep there, out of the cold. But I also had to find out where I was and the way to Dublin. I thought of myself being home just in time for Christmas. I decided that the best thing to do would be to sneak back into the village and have a look at the road signs. They'd never think that I'd be in the village. I trotted back the way that I had come. Within a short time I could see the dormo lights of St Joseph's. Every few minutes a car would zoom past on the road in search of me. The village was empty of people and no lights were on, not even the police station lights. I thought, it must be late. The rain now seemed to come down heavier than ever. I could barely see a thing as the rain spat itself onto the ground. I watched it rush along the roadside as if it was hurrying to get back to where it came from, every drop pushing and shoving each other, making a gushing guttery sound that filled the quiet village with activity. Like a fox jumping a stream, I lepped across the road, avoiding the deep puddles of water, onto the far side and out of the path of car lights and into the safety of small corners.

Moving from place to place on tiptoe, ears listening, eyes moving about like hawks watching for prey, I came to a parked car in the village. Its doors were locked. I stood back from the car, looking about. My foot shot forward. The fly window opened. I was moving fast, had to. Cars might come any minute. My hand reached in and down to the door handle. I opened the door and slid in, closing the door behind me. I lay face down on the seats listening for anything coming.

Nothing. I searched the car, got a flash lamp, screwdriver, keys, a coat. I put the coat over me. It was huge and warm. I switched on the lamp to see was there anything else, but nothing. I searched the pockets of the coat, found matches, butts, a hankie, some change. I sat there out of the rain watching it, listening to it. Cars passed, stopped, turned and went back the way they had come. I laughed, lit a cig and, although I couldn't drive I tried to start the car with the keys. It gave me something to do. I tried and tried but the thing wouldn't start so I just sat looking at the road. I could see them but they couldn't see me. I watched them get out of their cars. The Head Brother, McCann, had his green Vauxhall and Johnny Lamb had his car. They talked for a while. I couldn't hear what they were saying, but I knew they were looking for me. I made a bed between the passenger seat and the driver's seat and soon fell off to sleep.

The pram shed was cold. The only heat came from me and Lassie. We slept close together to keep warm, but a cold breeze kept sweeping in from under the door. I was woken the next morning by something pulling on my hair. At first I thought Lassie was biting my hair, but he wasn't. It was me ma's hand on my hair. I hadn't a chance.

'Come out you. You're never done making a show of me. But you'll do it no more.'

'I didn't do anything, Ma, I swear.'

'You took that meat from out of the kitchen to give to that bastarding dog. I had that meat kept to make sandwiches for your Uncle Francis and when I brought the chap back to the flat the meat was gone. You'll pay me for that meat.'

Ma had me by the neck all this time, reefing me around the

flats and screaming in temper. Lassie thought that we were playing and he started to bark and hop and run around the place.

'Let me go Ma. I didn't rob your meat. Somebody else must have taken it. It wasn't me,' I said, struggling to get free.

But me ma wouldn't let go of me. I got reefed up the stairs and onto the balcony.

'OK, OK, I can walk.' I could feel me ma loosening her grip on me and see Martina at the hall door waiting for me with a smirk upon her face. 'Put him straight into bed, Ma. He did take that meat.'

'I didn't, Martina, I swear.'

'You dangerous liar, you did take that meat. I saw you.'

It was now or never. I couldn't bear the thoughts of being kept in bed all day, so I pulled with all my strength and broke free of me ma's hand. Martina was standing stunned, shocked and too slow to move out of my way. As I passed her I couldn't resist reaching out my hand and giving her the palm of it straight into the kisser. I was inches past her when I heard the clatter and the yelp, and I was well out of the reach of both of them when I heard her cry, 'Did you see that, Ma?' I was already down the stairs and heading towards the gates of the flats.

'You little fucker, James,' Ma screamed, 'you have me heart broke. Let the police take you now and you won't get much meat where you're going, me boyo.'

Everybody was going off to work. I didn't know where I was going. It was too early in the morning anyway. So I just walked around St Stephen's Green with Lassie, waiting for it to open. When we did get in, gardeners chased us out again 'cause Lassie was chasing the ducks. I found a bit of rope and we went back in again. The gardener caught up with me.

'Why aren't you in school?' he asked.

'It's too early,' I said.

'Where do you live?'

'Connolly House.'

'What are you doing out at this hour of the morning?'

'I'm taking me dog for a walk.'

'What's his name?'

'Lassie O'Neill.'

'And what's your name?'

'James O'Neill.'

'Well James,' he said. 'Would you like to grow up to be a gardener?'

'No,' I said.

'Well then, you better be off to school and learn to be something else, isn't that right? Now go on out with you, off to school.'

I looked at him.

'Go on now, I know your father. I'll tell him. Go on son, go and learn something. You can't stay here. You'll get me into trouble, and here, take the dog with you, there's a good boy.'

I left the park by the Grafton Street gate, every now and again looking back at the gardener in his uniform and his walking stick behind his back, his big goggle eyes watching me to make sure that I went out the gate. Everybody called him Goggles because of his glasses, those big thick ones like the ends of milk bottles. When me and Lassie arrived at the school everybody was getting off the Ballyfermot buses.

'Where did you get the dog, Neiller?' one of them asked.

'I found him,' I said, 'and he's a great jumper.'

'Bring him into the school,' somebody shouted, 'seize him on the Master.'

I wasn't really listening to what they were saying to me. I

was too busy looking for Bracko, Peter Bracken, to come on the hop with me. I found him and, when he saw the dog, he was game. Off we went over to Francis Street School for Eamon Doyle. He came too. They both hid their school-bags down the basement of Jacob's biscuit factory. There was always a door open so it was easy to get in. It was easy to get push-bikes out of there as well, but it was always hard to get the biscuits.

After we hid the bags, we were off nicking anything that we could find. We got run out of most shops 'cause we were known. But we got some sweets and other things out of Woolworth's. I got a Batman car. None of us got any money and it was nearly two o'clock, so the only thing to do was to ask Christy Foley could we sell his papers for him, and he said yes. So we sold them and fucked off and spent the money on him. We bought chips and smokes, got our photos took, bought ice pops and ice cream. We bought loads of things until all the money was gone. Then we had to nick again 'cause Lassie was hungry.

Eamon Doyle said that he knew where there was a factory that had loads of cans of dog food up by the Naller and that it would be easy to nick some. So off we headed towards the factory, along the canal messing with parked cars and bikes and hiding ourselves from Lassie to see if he was a good tracker and could find us. He always did. So we rubbed his head and patted his back for him. Peter Bracken threw sticks for the dog into the water of the canal, but Lassie would not budge to go in after them.

'Bet you that bleeding dog can't swim,' he said.

'What do you mean?' I said. 'All dogs can swim.'

'Then, why doesn't he go in after the stick?'

"Cause it's not a duck. He only goes in after ducks. He's not

stupid, you know. Look, I'll bleeding show you.' I called
Lassie over and lifted him up with all my might. He was
heavy. I carried him over to the edge and threw him into the
water. He made a big splash, and then he was gone for a few
seconds. I thought that he was after drowning 'cause I could-
n't see him anywhere. Bracken was laughing and shouting,
'Yeah, he can swim like a rock, bleedin' submarine dog.'

Before Bracken could get the next word out of his mouth,
Lassie came into sight.

'Here Lassie, come on boy.' I called his name with delight.
'Watch this,' I said to Bracken and ran along the canal bank
calling Lassie's name. He swam like a speedboat after me.
Bracken and Doyle followed.

Lassie got out of the water and shook all the water off
himself.

'See,' I said, 'he's even a better swimmer than youse.'

Doyle led the way to the factory and the four of us sneaked
in past the man that was in the hut by the gate. When we got
inside, the place was packed high with boxes of Kitekat, Pal
and other pet food. We got behind the boxes and burst one
open. We took a few cans each and sneaked back out again.

We ran down the street towards Grand Canal Street and
when it was safe, we stopped and tried to open the cans. We
couldn't so we bashed them off the ground until they bursted
open. Eamon Doyle got his open first and he started to give it
to the dog. Lassie ate it from his hand. There was a nice smell
off it, I thought, watching Lassie mill into it.

'I wonder, can you eat that stuff?' I said to Bracken.

'Yeah,' said Eamon Doyle, 'it's like real meat.'

'Dare you to eat some so,' I said to Doyle.

'How much?' said Doyle.

'I bet you two bob.'

'You haven't got two bob,' he said.

'No,' I said, 'but when I get it, I'll give it to you.'

He said OK. Peter Bracken and I watched as Doyle took a lump from inside the can, put it into his mouth, chewed and swallowed it. Even Lassie was staring at him.

'That's two bob you owe me,' he said.

I was sure that he was going to drop dead, and I didn't want to be the one to have to go and tell his ma. 'Mrs Doyle, Eamon has been taken to hospital 'cause he ate a tin of dog food and collapsed.' But he didn't drop dead. Peter Bracken was falling about the place laughing calling Doyle 'Spot' and 'Rex' and running up and down the street calling, 'Here, Rover.' Doyle got mad and started throwing the other cans of dog food after Bracken, trying to split him, but Bracko was too slippery and Doyle gave up.

We weren't far from the Dogs and Cats Home so we decided to go there and try to rob one of the dogs from out of the cages. We could hear the cats and dogs and we could see some of them through the locked wire gate. An office sign hung on a door. Bracken stayed outside with Lassie 'cause he was a stray and the people in the home might have taken him away. Me and Doyle went into the office. There was a counter running along one side of the office. Behind it was a man and a woman. The woman came up and asked could she help us.

'Can we have a look around at the dogs to see if our dog is here? He's gone missing and we can't find him anywhere. We can't go home without him.'

'Well, of course you can,' said the woman. 'Now, tell me what's his name?'

'Lassie is his name, Miss.'

'Did he have any identification on him?'

'What, Miss?'

'Did he have a collar with his name and address on it?'

'No, Miss.'

'I see. What colour was he and what sort of dog?'

'Brown and white. He's a sheepdog.'

She went over to a drawer, took out a big book and went through it for a while. Then she came back.

'Well, I don't think that your Lassie is here.'

'Can we go in and have a look to see? We won't be long.'

Then she opened the glass door that was in front of us. It led out into the yard where all the dogs and cats were. 'Have a good look now and, if you find him, come back and let me know.'

The door closed behind us and we were left standing on our own.

'Jaysus, Eamon. There's millions of dogs.'

'Yeah, and fucking cats,' Eamon said. 'They should let the dogs eat the cats.'

We moved towards the cages of dogs, all sorts of dogs – pups, grown-up dogs, allers, terriers, boxers, Dobermans, small dogs, huge dogs, vicious dogs. They were all crying and barking, jumping about in their cages. We went over to them to pick one out. We had a good look before picking out the one that we wanted, a young Alsatian, gorgeous he was, licking our hands and all, a good sign that he liked us.

I kept nicks, looking out for anyone coming, while Eamon tried to break the lock and chain from the cage. The bleeding dogs must have thought that it was their birthday and they were all getting out or something because they all started to howl and bark altogether. It frightened me. I thought they were going mad to eat us and it nearly got us caught. The woman came tearing out of the office. I saw her just in time to warn Doyle.

'Oh, you must not go too near the cages, nor put your hands near to the dogs. They can be very vicious and bite the hand off you.'

'I'm sorry Miss, I didn't know. They look OK. We were just having a look for our own dog.'

'Well, I don't mind you having a look, but you must be careful.'

She left, but it was useless, any time we went to break the cages the dogs all started up again.

'Anyways,' Doyle said to me. 'You would want to be a gorilla to smash open them locks.'

We were going to have a look at the cats when we both noticed a Volkswagen van with a canvas back on it and went over near it to see was there anything in it. Both our heads moved around, making sure that we weren't being watched, as we walked to the van to get a good look inside. We both stood on the back bumper. I lifted up the canvas. We both looked behind once again.

It was the smell I got first, but I couldn't make it out. It wasn't until I turned to look into the van that I got what it was, the van was packed with dead dogs and dead cats. Some had their eyes open. You could see some of their teeth showing as if someone was pulling their mouths back to the full, all quiet and stiff. Me and Eamon got the fright of our lives, we jumped off the back of the van and ran back into the office. I was feeling kind of cold. Eamon looked white. The both of us wanted to get out of there as quick as we could. We both wanted to run but couldn't 'cause the people might think that we'd done something wrong and run after us.

'Well, did you find your dog?' the woman said to us with a smile on her face. Neither of us answered her.

'Maybe tomorrow,' she said, as we moved out the door.

Bracken wouldn't believe us. He wanted us to go back in with him to show him. He called us chicken because we wouldn't go back in with him.

'Bleeding right, we're chicken. Let's see you go in on your own. Go on, let's see you,' we both said, but he didn't. 'Come on, let's get out of here.'

Lassie was delighted to see me. He kept jumping up on me to lick my face. The sight of the dead dogs was still on my mind. I looked at Lassie and thought for a moment that, if the people in the Dogs and Cats Home caught him on his own, they might do the same thing to him.

'Come on, come on,' I shouted to the others.

We went down Mount Street together. There were a lot of the old tenement houses all boarded up and we talked about getting in to one of them to catch pigeons. You can always get pigeons in broken-down houses. But Lassie couldn't climb so we didn't go in, we just went on heading towards town. On the way Peter Bracken started calling out Lassie's name. He was calling Lassie's name but he was looking at Doyle.

'Are you calling me Lassie, Bracken?' Doyle said, ''cause if you are, I'll stick you all over the kip.'

'I'm not calling you anything. I was just calling the dog, I was. Lassie,' Bracken called again, looking straight at Doyle.

'I'm fucking warning you, Bracken. I'll bleeding smash you. Now, I'm telling you for the last time, shut your trap.'

We walked on past Merrion Square where all the museums are. We didn't bother going in. On the stalls outside Greene's Bookshop there was a big pile of books and there were some people going through them. We went over to have a look at the books, but we started messing with them. I picked up a book and threw it at Bracko. It missed and slid along the footpath. Somebody must have told the man in the shop 'cause he was out like a flash, holding a long pole in his hand, one of those poles that they use for pulling windows open.

'Youse little brats. I'll have the gardaí after youse.'

He was an oldish man. We told him to fuck off, hoping that he would chase us. We ran up Nassau Street, Peter up in front, booting the book around like a football. We could hear the man shouting after us: 'The guards are coming and I know every one of youse. Don't worry boys, I'll be handing them your names.'

We lashed along the street towards Grafton Street and St Stephen's Green as fast as we could, bumping into people, dashing out in front of cars. 'Have you any manners?' people would shout after us. 'God, it's disgraceful! They shouldn't be allowed roam the streets like that.' 'Where are their parents?' We didn't give a bollix, just kept running and laughing at them. We didn't care.

We took a short-cut through a side street and ended up in Wicklow Street. We stopped outside the Post Office in Anne Street. I used to be able to get letters out of the letter box by putting me hand and me arm through the slit. Once I got a letter with a pound note and a ten-bob note. But there were too many people around now to try to do it. But there was a fruit shop beside it and instead of trying to get the letters, we all looked in through the window at the fruit, waiting for our chance to grab the big bunch of grapes that was nearest the door on the right-hand side of the window. It was dead easy. Doyle kept watch. I reached my hand into the window, leaned a little bit further, just a little bit more, got them. 'Let's go.'

We strolled down Grafton Street, bursting juicy grapes in our mouths. I kept the bunch in my hand 'cause I was the one that got them, so I was the one that shared them out. Two for me and two for them, one each. Lassie didn't like grapes, so I was eating his share. Lassie kept on getting lost in the crowds walking the street. It was when I turned around to look for him that I noticed someone charging through the crowds of people, pushing them aside to get his hands on us. It was the man out of the fruit shop. He was like a madman. I screamed to the others to scarper. 'Here Lassie.' Everyone went different directions. We weren't thinking that anybody would follow us 'cause we were sure that nobody saw us take the grapes. I was out on the road now, running for my life down Grafton Street towards Trinity College, with half a bunch of grapes in one hand and the other half in me mouth. I could hear the man shouting and roaring at the people in the street to stop me. 'Stop him, hold that lad.'

Lassie was running alongside me now. I thought that was why nobody tried to stop me 'cause he was barking and jumping about, thinking that we were playing or something. So I ran on as fast as I could, trying to stuff the grapes into my mouth to get rid of them. I didn't want to throw them away. Now me mouth was stuffed with them.

I jumped in off the road and onto the path again, 'cause a car nearly knocked me down and all the other people in their cars started barping their horns at me to get in off the road. I should have stayed running along the road because when I got onto the footpath there were too many people and I couldn't move fast enough. As well as that, Lassie kept on getting himself lost in among the crowds so I had to wait for him.

The man's hand came from nowhere and so did his voice.

'If you swallow those grapes, I swear by Christ I will kill you. Do you understand?' He shook me. 'You little bastard. You won't steal from my shop again in a hurry, not when I'm finished with you, you won't.'

I couldn't see Lassie anywhere and all the people stopped

and gawked at me being pulled by the scruff of the neck back up Grafton Street. Every few steps he would stop and say to me: 'You'd better not swallow those grapes, do you hear me?'

I nodded my head, terrified at the thought of what the bastard was going to do with me. I was even terrified to open my mouth for fear the grapes might fall. I was sure that Christy Foley, whose newspapers we fucked off with, was going to walk down the street any minute and ask for his money. I was pulled by the neck, back up to the shop, in the door and down the steps into the basement. There was a pile of rubbish on the floor in one corner. The man pointed over to it.

'Now, get over there and spit every last drop of my grapes out of that mouth of yours and don't try anything for I'll be watching you.'

I didn't try a thing. I spat them all out onto the rubbish and looked over at him standing against the wall with his arms folded across his chest

'There, that's them all.'

He came across to me. 'Where's the rest of them?' he shouted. 'That's not them all. Come on, get the rest up.'

He frightened me and I started to cry.

'That's all I took, I swear, Mister. I won't do it again.'

He shook and shook me, screaming.

'I'll get them out of you before you leave this shop. I'll teach you that it is better to buy than to steal. Come on, get them out.'

I copped on to what he wanted me to do and I tried to vomit the rest of them out of my stomach. But fear would not let them go. I tried and tried, my eyes running with water from tears and trying to force myself to get sick. 'I can't. I'm sorry. They're stuck.'

I felt the force of his boot smash against my back. I hopped with pain and screamed. His hand came full force, smack against the back of my neck and his voice boomed at me to shut up and stop acting the baby. 'Now, get back up those stairs.' He brought me to the door and kicked me onto the street. 'Don't ever let me see you near this shop again, you or any of your friends.'

I wanted to run somewhere, anywhere, just to hide my face from the crowd of people that had stopped to look. I didn't run, not just yet anyway. I walked back out to Grafton Street, my head down to stop people looking at me crying. My neck felt burning hot and my back sore from his kick, and I was sad that Lassie was now gone and Doyle and Bracken were nowhere to be seen.

I wanted to go home to tell me ma what that bastard did to me, but couldn't. I wanted to get my big brother to fucking kill him but I didn't have one. I turned the corner into another street and ran ...

EIGHT

The noise from the pelting rain bashing on the roof of the car woke me. I felt cold, damp. The realization of what I had done began to dawn upon me. I had no idea of the time. The sky was grey and it was still pouring rain. I thought it might be better to give myself up, walk back into the school and say I was sorry. I could see the place from where I was sitting. It looked and felt even colder than I felt but I didn't care. I wanted to be caught. I wanted to cry to them, wanted to be held by warm hands.

I left the car and walked along the road, hoping that the next car would be the Head Brother's car and then I could get in and he would be glad to see me and he'd understand and wouldn't hit me or let anybody else hit me. I could see Kylemore Abbey and just above that the white statue of Jesus halfway up the mountainside. I didn't ask for his help 'cause I felt that he could see me now, 'cause I could see him and he would know how I felt. Anyway, I thought that it was better not to ask for his help 'cause then he'd be bound to give it.

I crossed onto the bridge, walked down the middle of it and stopped, looking up and down the road. There wasn't a thing in sight, no cars, no people, just the sound of the river. I leaned over the side and stood there staring into the water. Its sound felt like its strength and its strength gave it its speed. It seemed as if each current was trying to outpace the other in its frantic effort to get back to the sea. The rain was dropping from the clouds more heavily now. I could feel it splash onto my head, it ran down my face in small lines like tiny streams and sank into my clothes making them heavy and cold. The sound from the river grew loud and fierce as more and more drops of rain joined the endless race to find their place in the open sea. I stood there like a wet pigeon afeared to fly.

When I heard the sound of the car engine I didn't even bother to turn around to have a look. I didn't run, didn't hide. The horn from the car sounded. I turned my head around. I could see the driver lean over and the passenger door open. I walked slowly to the car, my body cold and my clothes soaked. Brother McCann was sitting at the wheel. I felt glad to see him. I felt that I could cry now 'cause he would understand. I sat into the car. It felt warm and dry. I watched the wipers chase the rain down off the windscreen. Brother McCann didn't say one word nor give me one look as he turned the car towards the school. In the time since I'd run away I'd only got three miles away from Letterfrack. It wasn't very far, I thought, as we drove along the road.

Then, out of the blue, Brother McCann said, 'Why did you run away, James?' I didn't look at him. I couldn't look at him, I just hoped that he would understand. I couldn't even answer him. I felt choked. It wouldn't come out. I turned to look at him. As I did, his hand came off the wheel, like an arrow leaving its bow, and sliced across my face. The dam could take no more. The tears bursted out. I cried and sobbed. The tears ran down my cheeks like the rain. I held my hands up to cover my face. The journey back didn't take very long. Again the

Brother asked me why I ran away. I didn't answer. The car pulled up inside the school. It was still early morning and the rest of the boys were yet to come down from the dormos.

'Come on, follow me,' he said.

We walked across the yard into the corridor, up the stairs and into my dormo. Everybody was lining up to wash. I could see Brother Michael pacing up and down the line. Then he looked down and saw me and Brother McCann and came down to us. I watched him and the boys that were in the line watched me. The boys in the line started to talk.

'Silence,' Brother Michael shouted up to them.

The talk stopped and Brother McCann left the dormo. Brother Michael gripped me by the shoulder and brought me to my bed.

'Wait here until the rest of the boys have finished and gone down into the yard. Stand there now, and don't move until I'm ready for you.'

I didn't move. I waited for what was coming to me, hoping that it would be quick. The waiting is always the worst and then it came.

The cane, leather, the strap, punch, clatter and kick, tears, hatred, pain. I am a man, no I'm a boy, a child, a thief, a little savage, running wild. Now it's over, I'm beaten. I'm clean of sin. The Brother smiles and claps his hands and I fall in.

After the beating I felt different. The tears stopped, everything had left me and now there was nothing – no love, no Ma, no Da, no Christmas holidays and no escape. I had to survive on my own, without the pack, pull down the shutters. I could sit with the big blokes now, because they knew that I wasn't going to tell anybody about the smokes that they had or what they were saying about girls and queers and all. I think they liked me 'cause they thought I was a madman after biting Joey

Finn's chest and escaping. They said only a madman would sit outside the school in a car. Joey Finn didn't bother me anymore. I wasn't afeared of him now because I knew that Tony Keane wouldn't go in for him again. If I hadn't got those beatings off the Brothers, the big fellas wouldn't have let me sit with them. I'd have been told to fuck off, but now they called me Madzer. That became my nickname but I didn't let everybody call me that, only the big fellas.

I was getting to know a lot of things about girls. I didn't really understand it all but I could picture it and I kind of knew where to put it. The big fellas talked all the time about girls and doing it with them. In the recreation hall one night one of them was telling a story about his bird givin' him a gobble and lettin him rub and hold her diddies, but she wouldn't drop her knickers.

'Not that it mattered,' he said. 'I got me prick between her chats. It was great.'

'Bleeding diddies are no use without the ride,' said his mate. 'Listen, pal. It's the bleedin' ride that counts.'

'Yeah, I know, but she's me mot and she's afeared I might put her up the pole.'

'Fuck putting her up the pole. Get the gee, and do a moonlight. There's more than one ride around. Ask Madzer.'

I was listening like a tape-recorder. 'Yeah, yeah. There's stacks,' I said, trying to look and sound as if I knew it all. Best to sound like half an idiot that knows something, than a whole idiot that knows fuck-all. When I was on my own, I used to think about it a lot and sometimes I really wished I could do it, but then I didn't really know what to do and I couldn't ask the big boys how it was done. I just listened and listened and watched. Sometimes they would talk about Fitzgerald and the watchman. 'They're riding and queering each other,' they would say. Again, I couldn't imagine just exactly what they were doing or how they could be doing it to each other. All the same, the thoughts of that gave me a funny feeling. Maybe, maybe you can do it with another boy, I wondered. I didn't get into much trouble hanging around with the big blokes; it was my mind that got into a terrible mess. My imagination ran wild thinking that if you put it between her legs, you'd have done it. I was sure that that was where to put it. I felt alone. The big boys were just the cover I had to have. It made the other boys think I was hard. I had to pretend that I was a tough fella, battling on against whatever, when really the only battle that was going on was within myself, a battle I didn't know nor understand and it was growing. I had to keep it to myself, no other way – the hard side for the school, the other side I kept to myself.

It was a week before all the boys were going home for their Christmas holidays. Me and Patrick Behan were working in the drying room of the laundry, folding up the sheets. Mrs Kelly had gone home and left us there to finish off a couple of sheets. The sheets were big and to fold them I would take one end and he would take the other. We had to hold out the sheet, fold it over three times, then walk towards each other to bring the two ends together, then fold it once again, him taking the bottom half and me the top. Patrick was a bit older than me, twelve maybe.

We were working away, not saying a word to each other, just the two of us, but there was something going on in his mind. I could sense it but didn't know what it was. Any time we came close together to fold the sheets, he'd look straight into my face and wouldn't stop looking. Then it dawned on me what was going on. The thought of it sent messages all over my body, my face flushed, my heart began to quicken and there was nothing I could do about it. I felt shy, uneasy and embarrassed. My face felt as if you could fry an egg on it. I wanted to say something but I couldn't. This feeling that was usually only inside of me was now hovering in the air. I tried to get my mind to fight what was happening to my private, but it wouldn't work. I hoped Patrick might say something soon. Half of me wanted him to say what I was thinking, the other half wanted him to say something different. It wasn't the first time that things like this had happened, but at those times, Mrs Kelly would be around and it lasted no longer than a second, but she wasn't here now and it was well past a second. Maybe ... maybe he only wants to know what the big fellas do be talking about, and maybe I'd like to tell him that I know what it's all about. No, I thought, if he wanted to know, he would ask.

We took the last sheet from the table and began to fold it slowly. My insides felt as if they were melting, and, in my short trousers, I could feel my private twitching. I tried everything but I couldn't stop it growing. I began to turn my head in every direction, looked everywhere. I could see my private stick out in front of me. He couldn't see it, but I was afeared that he might. The only thing that stopped him from seeing it was the sheet that we both held between us, ready for its final fold.

'I mustn't let him fold the sheet,' I thought, ''cause, if he does, then he'll see, and if he does, he'll think I'm a queer.'

I wanted the sheet to hide my horn, so he couldn't see it. But he wouldn't let go of the sheet.

'Let go, will you. Look, I want the sheet for something,' I said, looking down at the floor. He didn't answer. I looked up at him. 'Are you going to give me the sheet?' I said, once again, in near-panic.

'You want to do it, don't you?' he said.

'Do what?' I said back, trying to pull the sheet from his hands.

'With somebody,' he said.

'Do what with somebody? Gimme the bleedin' sheet, will ya.'

'You know what I mean, doing it together with somebody. You know!'

'Give me the bleedin' thing.'

'Get one off the table, why don't you? What do you want this sheet for?'

He pulled the sheet from my hands. I turned around as quickly as I could to grab one from the table. But it was too late. Before my hand even reached the table, the words hit my ears.

'You're on a horn. I can see it. You do want to do it, don't you?'

Neither of us said anything for a moment, then he spoke.

'Did you ever do it with anybody before?'

'No,' I said.

'Did you?' still not looking at him and trying to get myself back together.

'Will we do it together?' he said, laughing and turning away.

The laugh made me feel OK. I picked up another sheet from the table and threw it at him, running for the door.

'Now you got two sheets, you can send them home to your ma,' I said and laughed.

Before I could get the door opened, he started to throw the sheets back at me, some hit me, others just opened up and sailed to the floor like parachutes. I ducked out of the way from the next load that came at me and grabbed a pile to throw back at him. Back and forth the sheets sailed across the room. Back and forth until there were no sheets left on the table, no sheets left on the shelves, back and forth till the floor was knee deep with white sheets.

We stopped. No sheets to throw. No more words to say. It didn't matter now. We both stood there, looking at the sheet-covered floor, trying for something to make it alright. We moved towards each other, as if the other was not there, trying to make it happen as if by accident. Now, facing each other, not knowing what to do, each hoping that the other would make the first move, I could see his private, standing straight and still in his pants no bigger than mine. Closer, closer until the air that I was breathing in was the breath that he was breathing out, closer and closer like never before. Then we mingled and tangled with the white sheets on the floor, twisting and turning, his hands on my bum and I've got his private between my finger and thumb, just touching, not looking, much too shy. The girl I dreamed of became the laundry boy. Rolling and tumbling in our bed made from sheets, shush, someone's coming and we jump to our feet. Quickly, quickly, let's get the sheets back all neat.

'There, we did it,' Patrick said.

'Yeah, I hope nobody saw us. Do you think anybody will find out?'

'We better not tell anybody,' Patrick said.

'I won't,' I said.

'Neither will I,' Patrick said.

'Let's finish off the sheets.'

We folded them over without talking, without looking or touching except on our last sheet, when we looked at each other for a moment. I laughed, then we both laughed.

I sat up in my bed and watched the lads fold up their bedclothes, everything stripped off in seconds and placed neatly at the top of their beds. I could see that it was still dark outside and could hear the sound from the engines of the buses waiting to take the boys off on their journey home for Christmas. Now and again the engines would give a roar, as if telling the boys to hurry on. All the beds stood bare and looked as if nobody had slept in them. As the boys lined up against the wall in single file, they were smiling and laughing. Seeing them being happy, I longed to be going with them. Even Brother Michael seemed happy. A hush came over the boys as the line started to leave the dormo. I could hear the clatter of feet on the stairs, then the noise subsided and a loneliness descended onto the dormo like a rolling fog. There were a few other boys in the dormo with me. We'd all be staying at the school for Christmas.

I got out of my bed and climbed up onto the window-sill to watch the buses take off. I could hardly see a thing. The window-pane was frosted on the outside. The figures moved about down below, lit by the headlamps of the buses. Voices with words that I couldn't make out and shadows big as giants being cast by the light from the buses all across the yard. I rubbed the window-pane with my warm hand. It got cold. I wrapped my hand in my pyjama sleeve and wiped away the condensation. I could see better now, peeking out into the early morning blackness. It was snowing. I could see it as it fell into the path of the headlamps. Everybody was on board now, sitting, waiting for the wheels to turn. Some of the lads waved up to the windows, to us.

'I hope youse bastards bleeding crash,' somebody shouted from behind me.

The bus pulled off, moving slowly along the narrow road between the workshops and the playing yard. The lads around me looked sad. I felt sad. Some got down from the windows and back into their beds. I sat and watched until the tail-lights from the buses became like a lighted cigarette, growing smaller in the distance. And then no more. I was glad they were out of sight. The next time, I thought to myself, I'll be going.

I jumped down. The boys in the dormo were running all over the place now, messing, turning beds onto the floor. There were no Brothers about, and no sign of one coming, so fuck it, I joined in. Splinter Spillane lay face down in his bed, still and soundless. We crept nearer and nearer to him with a plan to push him out onto the floor. We were sure that he was asleep. Then, all at once, we pounced on him, screaming and yelling but he wasn't asleep. He jumped up before we had time to do anything.

'Fuck off, yez bleedin' swines. Leave me alone.' His face was red and the tears splashed out from his twisted eyes. 'Do yez hear? Leave me alone.'

I nearly burst out laughing at him 'cause he looked so funny, but I didn't. He was crying 'cause he didn't get home. Anyway, there was no time to laugh because the lads had turned to my bed and were wrecking it. I dashed over to stop them, but there was no point, the Jaysus bed was all over the dump. I gathered everything back onto the bed. Nobody noticed that the lads from St Joseph's had slipped into our dormo, armed to the hilt with knotted towels, pillow cases full of soap, cups of water, the lot. We were caught unawares and were bet up and down the dormo.

The school became very quiet. The mass sound of everybody together had gone. All that was left was about thirty between the two dormos, even some of the Brothers had gone. As Christmas Day got near, I got cards from me brothers and sisters and me ma sent me down a parcel of things. I sent cards home saying that I was OK and that I would see them on my summer holidays. Some of the boys didn't get letters or cards. The Brothers used give them to them, as well as sweets and other things. I loved getting letters and cards from home. The boys who didn't must have felt awful. Some of them said they had no ma or da. The tree, with all its colour, decoration, lights and chains stood at the bottom of the dining-hall, but it didn't look right. It was odd. All the tables were bare except for the few that we sat at, all bunched together at the top of the hall, and at the bottom, near the door, stood our Christmas tree. No one around it, just empty tables and the echo of our voices in the empty spaces.

I drained the last drop of tea from my cup and watched how the lights on the tree flickered on and off and then wondered at the size of the tree. God, I'd never be able to carry that for me ma. I could carry two small ones, but not one that big. It is a good job that she only buys small ones, I thought. At Christmastime at home, I'd help me ma carry the trees from the flats up to Camden Street to sell at her stall. Pushing and shoving, dragging trees up and down the street, I hated doing it. Every few yards I used to have to stop and bite big pine splinters out of my hands. I felt like a Molly too, bringing a load up in the pram because all the girls in the flats would be looking at me. Sometimes the trees would fall off the pram and roll onto the middle of the road and the whole street would come to a stop, busmen screaming their heads off at me, cars barping their horns. Everybody looking to see what was going on, and there I'd be out in the middle of the road, trying to get the bastarding trees back onto the pram, me hands filled with splinters. Then, when I got them to me ma, she would stand there with a mad look in her eye.

'You!' she'd say, 'I sent you for those trees over an hour ago.

I could have had them sold. Jaysus, Mary and Joseph. What did I rear?'

Everybody walking by would stare at me ma as if she was gone off the nut or drunk or something. Often I'd just dump the trees with her and run before she had time to say, 'James, run down again to the flats and bring me up a half-dozen middling size trees and that will be all. That's a good boy,' I'd already be halfway down Grafton Street.

Last Christmas Eve the morning was crisp, and the sharp, cold wind tossed my hair about and whistled through the trees that stood against the railings and the flats. They ran half the length of the railings and were seven to eight deep. A pine forest slap bang in the middle of Dublin. Me ma was taking fruit and veg and loading them onto the pram. My job was to get all the small trees out and bring them up to the stall. I didn't mind so much because everybody in the flats was asleep. Nobody would be gawking at me and me ma was in good humour, she was humming. In I went, into the thick of the forest and had pulled about a dozen small trees when I noticed me ma talking to the Corpo caretaker. I stopped and went up and stood beside me ma. He was telling me ma that the yard in Connolly House was built to provide a playground and that, on the orders from his head office, the trees must be removed, that there were that many trees in the flats, you would have to cut your way in with an axe.

'Now you just hold on there and let me tell you something,' Ma said to the Corpo man. 'It's a livin' I make from those trees to feed and clothe my children because there's nobody else going to do it for me. I earn my living, not like you, mooching drink morning, noon and night, off those who are nothing but moochers themselves. So, go on off with you now, fuck off back to the public house. I have my livin' to make.'

'Ah, Mrs O'Neill,' he said, 'sure I'm only doing what I'm told to do. That's me job. I have a living to make as well, you know.'

'Well, I'm telling you now, those trees are staying where they are until such time as I'm fit and ready to move them. Sure, come 'ere. What child would want to play in a kip like this? Certainly not your boss's children anyway. Go on now. Off with you. I have work to do. No doubt you haven't.'

Not knowing what to say, the Corpo man moved off in a kind of slippery awkward way. I looked up at me ma's face as she loaded the last box of tomatoes onto the pram. She began to hum again and I started to hum too 'cause I was glad, really glad, that she was me ma.

Christmas morning at the school, we all went to Mass. The church was full, the boys from the school sat on one side of the church, all dressed in suits, the people from the village sat on the other side. I saw Johnny Lamb there and the watchman and Mrs Kelly and her husband. The Brothers were sitting to the side of the altar. Some of the village kids sneaked stares over at us, but the rest of the people kept their eyes on the priest.

The Mass ended and we were told to go in peace but we had to wait till everybody from the village had left the church, then we went in single file down the steps and into the yard to wait for our breakfast. The tables were laid out nice with little presents at each place, and a Christmas card attached. We said our grace before meals and ripped open the presents, hoping that there might be a smoke or two in there somewhere, but there were none, just sweets, pens, colouring books and comics. After breakfast we dossed about the yard, talked about what each other had got, stuffed ourselves with all kinds of sweets and had a football match.

Then we went on our walk with the Brothers, wandering along the road, no straight lines, no one telling anyone else what to do, moving along like stray cattle. Smiling faces beamed out through a car window. We smiled back and waved our hands as they passed us. But nobody took their eyes off the road for very long for fear of missing the butt ends of the cigs that lay along the road. We rested at the bridge by Kylemore Abbey, stood there and dropped stones into the river, listened to its sound and watched as the ripples widened their circle across the breadth of the river. My eyes followed the river and its swiftness, and wished it would take me away. We strolled back along toward the school, slowly, lazily. The air from some of the balloons that hung on the Christmas tree had somehow escaped and those that were left hung from the tree, lifeless. We sat for our Christmas dinner and ate until we could eat no more. Roast spuds, turkey, mounds of custard and jelly, fruit. I felt that I was going to burst. Something was happening down the other end of the table. At first I thought that someone had spilt a cup of tea or something, but they hadn't – it was Splinter Spillane vomiting. One hand was covering his mouth but still the sick spurted out, splashed all over the place, down the front of his shirt. There was no sign of him getting away from the table.

'Get bleeding away from the table, ya dirt bird. Ya better not get dirty dick on me,' said Ryaner, a look of disgust on his face. Splinter paid no heed. He must have been rigged up to a sick bank 'cause he was still spewing up. Brother Byrne came rushing out from the kitchen, told Splinter to bend his stomach, not to move and to stay that way. Then the Brother went back into the kitchen.

'Here, Madzer, get up there and get some paper to cover that sick,' said Ryaner to me, laughing.

'Fuck off, will ya. Let him do it himself,' I said.

The Brother was out in a flash carrying a bucket and mop. Splinter was OK now and the Brother told him to clean it all up. We watched him mop up the sick and then, when the mop was caked with sick, he squeezed the bleeding thing with his hands into the bucket. The whole gang of us nearly vomited when he did that. Before he could do it again, everyone was shouting at him.

'You gickna.' 'You dirty stinking muck lark.' 'Ya filth pigeon, ya.' Ryaner called out, 'And your oul' one's a big dirt bird too.'

That was it. The mop exploded onto the table, sending cups, knives, forks, plates into every direction. Splinter was screaming and shouting at everyone to leave him alone. There was a scatter from the tables. The bucket of hand-squeezed sick hit another table, sending piles of broken plates and cups into the air. Splinter ran and grabbed the mop from the table and the thoughts of getting a sick-mop in the mush sent us running down behind the Christmas tree. Splinter ran around screaming, turning over tables. Then he made a go at Ryaner. Ryaner ducked to avoid the mop, came back up as quick as lightning, kicking Splinter to the deck with a boot into the stomach.

Brother Byrne pulled Ryaner off Splinter and held the both of them by the scruffs of their necks. He told the rest of us to get back to our places and to try to stop being animals for at least one day of our lives. We went back, sat at our tables and held our noses while Ryaner and Splinter were brought into the kitchen by Brother Byrne. Splinter walked doubled over, holding his guts.

We were brought over to the rec. hall to watch the Christmas films. The first film was finished and the second had just begun when Ryaner and Splinter came into the hall. We all turned around to have a look at them to see if anything had happened, but the *Old Mother Reilly* film was miles more interesting. So we all got back into it. All the films they showed us were short ones and as old as the hills. When they had shown us all fifteen films, it was time for our tea and, after that, we watched TV, played cards and rings, ate sweets, watched more RTÉ. I sat on my own for a while and thought about home, thought about the Christmas party that I had gone to at the police station the year before. The picture of it came clearly, my sister Sue bringing me by the hand down to Pearse Street cop-shop. The big gang of kids from all around the flats and neighbourhood standing outside, the policemen telling everybody to get into line or they wouldn't be getting in at all. Sue moved right to the top of the queue.

'How are ya?' she said to the cop.

'Sure there you are, Sue. It's yourself. Are you coming to hand yourself in or what? Changing your ways?'

'Yeah, gave it up, working in a convent now.'

'You're alright, cleaning it out would be more your line,' he said back.

Sue didn't answer him.

'James has got his ticket to go to your party, so take care of him for a while,' she said pushing me into the top of the queue. 'Mind him now, 'cause he's very wild.'

'Well,' said the policeman. 'There is a pair of youse in it. Go on, in you go.'

The gang of us were brought by the policeman into a big room. Red lino covered the floor and along the middle of the room was a long table, full of cakes, hats and sweets. Balloons and Christmas chains hung from the wall to the ceiling. Nothing on the table had been touched by any of us. We stood around and looked at it. If it had been any place else, the table would have been emptied before you could blink, but not in a police station with the police standing there, looking at you. A priest came into the room. 'Happy Christmas, boys and girls,' he said to us. Then he went among us patting us on the head. 'Good children, come on now and enjoy yourselves.'

We milled into the grub. A policewoman opened bottles of orange for us and handed them around.

'Now, when you have all that drunk, I'll give you another one,' she said as she handed me a bottle of orange, but I didn't want orange. I wanted raspberry. I sat up on the back of the chair looking around to see if I could see a place to dump it and then bring her back the empty bottle. There was a girl beside me with her coat on, so I poured the drink into her hood. She screamed the place down and before I had time to get rid of the bottle, the policewoman grabbed me by the hand, took the bottle from me, and slapped me across the back of the hand, saying, 'That's a very naughty thing to do.' I just looked at her. 'Do you hear me?' I said nothing. 'Right, if I catch you doing that naughty thing again, I'll have you sent home.'

The priest must have overheard her giving out to me. He came over to me, rubbed my head and said: 'Now James, if you can sing me a song on your own, there's a pound note here in my hand, and it will be yours.' I looked up at him. 'Go on,' he said, 'Off you go. Hushhhhhh.'

I sang a song. The priest stood by my side humming the tune. Halfway through the song, he took my hand and held it. Then he slipped the note from his hand to mine. I kept singing and looking around the room at everybody. Then I slipped the note into my pocket. The song finished. I got a big cheer. All the gang from the flats clapped and laughed. When everybody else had sung their song, it was time to leave and, as a treat, they drove us home in police cars. In the car I was in, there was about six of us.

'Ah, go faster, go on, break the lights. Put on the blue lamp.' 'Ah go on, Sir, just for a minute.'

'Ah, come on now boys, leave that window closed,' shouted one of the policemen.

We came up Dame Street, took a short-cut and on up through South William Street, up Mercer's Hill and into Mercer Street; all the grannys that were standing at the street corner yappin' to each other got the shock of their lives. As we passed them by, we all screamed out of the window at them. The cops laughed.

The police car stopped outside the flats. 'Out yez get.'

'Ah go on. Give us another jaunt around the block, will ya?' I said to the policeman.

'Come now, out with ye. Sure it won't be long until we will be chasing you about the place, trying to get ye into it.'

We got out and I dashed up the stairs to the house to tell me ma about winning the pound note. Me ma was sitting at the fire and some of me brothers and sisters were watching the telly. 'Here, Ma, look what I got off the priest at the party. A pound.' I took the money out of my pocket without looking at it and showed it to me ma.

'That's not a pound note you eejit. That's a fiver.'

I looked at it for the first time. Jaysus, it was! But before I could get it back, it had gone into me ma's pocket.

'I'll hold onto that for you. You can put it towards your Christmas shoes.'

'Can I go out to play for a while, Ma?' I said.

'OK, be back here in half an hour.'

I sat on the steps raging that I hadn't looked at the money when I'd got it. And the priest, I thought to myself, telling me it was a pound. A priest, telling a lie, they're supposed to not do anything wrong. Maybe he made a mistake, I thought.

I sat there in the rec. hall until it was time to go to bed. That night I just slept. Christmas Day had passed, and things got back to normal. Most of the boys that got out for Christmas came back, but a few didn't. New boys were sent to the school. The school was always full but more boys kept coming. Slowly the wind calmed, the rain eased. The Brothers took away our extra blankets, gave us white tee-shirts and sandals and sent us to rake the hay.

NINE

The spring sun shone. I sat in the yard, my back against the wall. On either side of me sat Tobias and Hamid Reid. They were both black. They were sent down to Letterfrack from Artane for breaking out all the time. The last time they did a bunk they took about thirty other boys with them and went on a spree, nicking everything, until they were nicked driving a huge lorry down Benburb Street. They had both been locked up since they were babies, going from one orphanage to another, from the nuns to the Brothers, always together. Not many blokes bugged them or slagged their colour 'cause they were both good scrappers, but that didn't stop the Brothers from lashing them all the time.

We sat there in the sun, not saying much to each other, watching the rest of the boys walk around the yard. Brother Byrne came into the yard and took out his packet of twenty Sweet Afton, slowly, as if he knew that we were watching him, our tongues hanging from our mouths, gumming for a smoke. He placed the cig in between his upper and lower lips, while at the same time depositing the pack of nineteen Sweet Afton deep into his pocket. He took out a silver-coloured lighter and lit the cigarette.

'I hope it chokes him.' I said, but he couldn't hear me 'cause I said it under my breath. The smoke rushed out from his nostrils and mouth and away out into the open, while the cigarette, now in his right hand, sat lazily between the two middle fingers, smouldering. He took another puff.

'Look,' said Joe. 'The bastard doesn't even know how to smoke.

'He's only smoking 'cause he gets the poxy things for nothing,' Tobias said.

We watched almost in tears as the Brother stood on the half-smoked Sweet Afton.

'The bastard,' said Tobias, 'I hope he dies roasting.'

The sun got a little hotter and the activity in the yard came to a standstill with everybody sitting or lying like lazy dogs out in the sun. I waited till Brother Byrne drifted off and I slipped out of the yard.

I climbed the hillside that led up to the hayfield, watching my step as I got higher 'cause the nettles were everywhere like booby traps. The thick brown cakes of cow dung lay all along the pathway. There wasn't a Brother in sight so I decided to go on a wander about the hayfield. I stood at the top of the field, a good safe distance away from the few cows that were wandering about, chewing the grass and stopping now and again to look lazily over at me with one of those looks cows give you as if you are not there. At my back was the Atlantic. I felt its breeze glide through my hair, watched it toss the grass about as if at play. Across the field, hidden by overgrown bushes, ran a small river. I moved towards it, watching a cow beat the flies off his back with his tail. I jumped a small iron fence, fought through a thick bush of old trees that twisted and curled like snakes wrapped around each other. I'd never been here before. Excitement crept over me. Nobody knew where I was.

I stepped carefully onto the moss-covered stones that sat looking out of the water and sprang from one to the other, making sure that my socks and sandals didn't get wet, until I reached the far side. I lay down on my belly and drank from the side of the river. The taste of ice-cool water in my mouth was beautiful. I rolled up my sleeves and plunged my hands in, scooping up handfuls of water and letting it fall back in, splashing. Then, thinking that there might be fish in the river, I stopped, held my breath for a while, thinking that the fishes might think that I'd gone and that it was safe to swim again. And if they did, then I could grab one and keep it in the laundry. No fish came. I sat up, took off my sandals and my socks, waited until I got up the nerve, then plunged my feet right into the cold water. The shock sent the heat from my feet right through me, and out through my head. I lay back, resting upon my arms, twirling my feet around in the water.

I lay there, thinking of nothing, feeling the water tickling my toes. I closed my eyes, water moving past my feet downstream, carrying me gently in its stride. Daydreaming of the vast world of the fishes swimming underneath me, watching the free world of the birds floating above me. The sun melts me, forms me into vapour, breathes life into me, makes me a cloud. I move playfully through the sky.

That night it rained, not much, just a little bit. I sat in my bed looking at it and listening to it. The rattle of paper broke my listening to the rain. The *Dandy* was thrown onto my bed from another bed on my left and the voice called, 'Pass it on.' I did, giving it to the boy in front of me. I lay back, my head on my pillow, and hummed to the song that came out from the radio and watched my toes move to the rhythm of the music. 'Radio Luxembourg 208. News headlines. American B-52 bombers carried out heavy bombing on many guerrilla camps inside Vietnam today. Reports indicate direct hits and up to one hundred guerrillas killed. Now back to the sound of summer.' 'Gorillas, why are they killing gorillas?' I thought to myself. I couldn't figure it out.

I listened to the music. It was a good song and I could hear some of the boys at the back of the dormo singing along with it, 'Summertime and the living is easy, fish are jumpin' and the cotton is high. Your daddy's rich and your mamma's good lookin', so hush little baby, don't you cry.' Getting sleepy, I pulled the blankets up over my head, closed my eyes, listened for a while longer. 'One of these mornings, you're gonna rise up early, you're gonna spread your wings and reach to the sky ...' Then I fell asleep.

Dear Ma and Da and Family,

Just a word to tell you that I'm getting on OK. I got your last letter and the fiver, thanks. The sun is shining down here. How is everyone at home. Tell everybody that I was wondering about them. Ma, I'll never rob another bike again. The Brother told me that he'll get me a job on a messenger bike when I go home. Hey Ma, will you come down to see me soon please. Well, Ma, that's all I can think of for now. But will you send us something down to spend. Tell me brothers and sisters and all the people in the flats that I will see them soon, and me Aunt as well.

All my love to all the family, James. XXX

We were in class and when we'd finished writing our letters home, Brother Michael showed us all how to do an experiment. He took a jamjar and moss from his desk, told one of the boys to go out and half fill the jamjar with water. When it was brought back, Brother Michael put the green moss into the jar of water, then carefully put blotting-paper neatly around the inside of the jar. Then he asked one of the boys, 'What am I doing?' The boy stood up in his bench, dumbfounded. 'Well?' said Brother Michael. 'What am I doing?'

'Putting green stuff into a jar, Brother.'

The duster shot through the air and hit the boy right in the mush, sending chalk dust all over the classroom.

'So I'm just putting green stuff into a jar, am I? Stand face against that wall till you wake up. Burke, what am I doing?'

'You're experimenting, Brother.'

The jamjar stood on top of Brother Michael's desk, full of blotting-paper, half-full of water and full with green moss. Then Brother Michael took out a packet of peas. Opening them, he took one out, carefully placing it into the jar, leaving it to rest between the inside of the blotting-paper and the glass. He leaned back from it, folded his arms across his chest. I was bored with the experiment. I didn't care what it was.

'Two shillings for the first boy that tells me what it is.'

Everybody's hand went up, 'Brother.' 'Brother, Brother.' 'Brother.' 'Sir, I'll tell ya, Brother.' 'Sir, I know.' Even the fella that had his face to the wall had his hand up. Brother Michael asked about ten of us for the answer; one half said it was going to be a tree and the other half said it would be a flower.

'So you think it may be a tree or a flower?' he said coldly. His voice brought an icy tension over the class. 'Your Irish books, page fifteen, bottom of the page. Keane, commence reading,' said Brother Michael.

We went for our Irish books like cowboys to the draw in a deadly gunfight. Tension hung around our heads.

'Well Mr Keane, what's keeping you, eh?' asked Brother Michael.

'I can't find the page, Brother,' pleaded Keaner.

'You can't find the page. And what page might you be looking for? Well?'

'I don't know, Brother.'

'Spillane, what page are we on?' asked Brother Michael, his eyes staring mercilessly at Keaner.

'The bottom of page fifteen, Brother,' said Splinter Spillane, his voice nervous.

'Spillane,' said Brother Michael, 'Go out to the wash-hand basin and fill a bucket of water. Bring it and some soap back here.'

I could feel the panic rage around me. Boys were checking their books to see was it page fifteen, rechecking, their minds beginning to get unsure, thinking, yes it must be fifteen he asked for, but what is he sending Splinter out for a bucket of water for? Was Splinter right or wrong? I prayed quietly to myself. I didn't look but I was sure the hair was standing on everybody's head.

We waited. Then in came Splinter carrying the water. He stood by the Brother's desk, awaiting his instructions. Brother Michael walked down the narrow aisle that separated the rows of desks. Nobody turned around when they heard the yelps, the ouchs and ahs. We were too busy thanking God that it was not one of us. Keaner was brought in front of the class, led by the ear and standing on his tippy-toes like a ballet dancer.

'Spillane, bring the water over here.'

Spillane moved towards the Brother and stopped. Holding

Keaner by the ear with one hand, the Brother plunged the other into the water and began to wash Keaner's ear roughly. Keaner's face went bright red.

'If you don't wash your ears in the morning, how do you expect to hear what I'm saying? Is that right Mr Keane?'

'Yes Brother, that's right, Brother,' said Keaner.

'Now,' Brother Michael screamed into Keaner's ear. He grabbed him between the legs and Keaner screamed in pain. 'Let's ...' The bell sounded. Class was over, it was time for work. Brother Michael looked disappointed. 'Tomorrow, Mr Keane,' he said.

Gratefully we placed our Irish books under our desks, stood up, said our prayers and left the classroom in single file. We walked along the corridor and out into the playing yard, filling it up, class after class, line after line, boy after boy. Running, walking, dreaming, roaring, screaming, pushing, shoving. We played like children in the school yard until the Brother clapped his hands to fall into line for work and we stood there in the hot sun facing the Brothers and Johnny Lamb. Brother Moy called out the orders: 'Cleaners fall out, tailors, bootmakers ...' I listened, but he didn't call out the laundry. Brother Moy left and Lamb took charge of those of us who were left.

'Right lads, the hayfield. Single file on the double!'

The hayfield was covered with hay freshly cut by the tractor.

'Stretch out along the top of the field in a straight line and get to it,' Lamb shouted at us.

We had to bend our backs over and move up the field, raking up the hay with our fingers. The human comb moved along the field pushing up the hay in its path, leaving the field behind green and spotless. My back was sore, my nose clogged with hay dust. Lamb was watching us to make sure that none of the hay was left behind. If there was, he would wallop you with a stick that he had in his hand. It was always best to do the raking right, 'cause if you didn't, you would leave a trail of hay behind pointing right at you, and that was all he needed to lash the legs from under you and then make you do the field on your own. Now and again a field mouse would dart away in terror at the army of oncoming fingers; sometimes one of the lads would dash after it just for a joke.

I could feel the sun scorching my neck as we moved along. I tasted the salty sweat that watered my face. I wanted to scratch all over from the dusty dry hay, feeling thirsty, needing a rest. Another few minutes, maybe, I thought. We worked until we stood behind a mountain of hay, then rested. My body fell like jelly upon the soft hay. The sun was fading. The haystacks we'd built stood high. We'd tied them with ropes. We listened for Lamb's command to fall into line, to march like a band back to the school. We marched, I with an itch in me back, my lips all dry, blistered and cracked.

Back in the schoolyard we lined up against the jax wall, two lines straight as arrows. Brother Michael stood at one end of us, Brother Moy at the other, and Brother Byrne in the middle of the line. Out we moved from the school towards the Atlantic Ocean, swimming-knicks and towel under the arm. The water was freezing. I stood at the edge, my toes just barely touching the water, but I knew that I would have to get in sooner or later. Everybody had to get in, whether he could swim or not, and if you didn't get in then the Brothers would throw you in, and if they didn't get you then the lads would. I could hear the roars and screams of the fellas that were getting thrown in and in a split second I took a deep breath and a dicky dive into the water. Before long we were all showing off to each other, as to who was the best swimmer or who could stay under the longest. Under the water Keaner and Ballyer were grabbing blokes by the legs and pulling them down and the Brothers couldn't see a thing.

'If you wanted to escape,' said Splinter Spillane, 'You could swim the breaststroke from here to Dublin.'

'Go away, you fucking eejit, the only breaststroke you ever did was when you pissed in the bed,' said Ryaner. 'C'mon Madzer,' he said grabbing me by me privates, 'let's go out to the pole.'

I struggled free, but Ryaner came after me. I dived like a submarine and swam with all my strength towards the rocky land. I looked back and under the water I saw Keaner's legs swimming towards me and Ryaner's swimming away. My eyes open, my lips sealed, my lungs still, I moved easily through the water, now watching the feet of the other boys as they swam about above me. Their hands and arms were spread out, moving non-stop to keep themselves afloat. Armies of hands, arms and legs, making millions and millions of splashes that sent the fishes dashing. I wish you could see me, Ma, in the salty-watered sea, Ma, where the smooth-faced stones lie silently like bones, and the tiny red crabs make them their homes. I'm swimming in the ocean, Da. My back against the sky.

The Brothers clapped and everyone got out of the water. The Brothers were shouting at us to hurry up. I sat down to put on my socks and sandals. The summer breeze was sweeping down on us, the sun sinking deeper, miles out at sea. The midget flies were out now, buzzing about in gangs of millions. I fastened my sandals and walked up to where the Boys were forming into two lines. Me and Keaner were paired off, with Ballyer and Ryaner in front of us.

'Do you think you'd be able to swim from here to Dublin?' asked Ballyer.

'Na, sharks'd eat you,' said Keaner.

'You could probably do the dead man's float,' I said, 'float on the water, like.'

'Na,' said Keaner again pointing towards the mountains. 'The only way out of this place is that way.'

'Nobody ever made it back to Dublin,' Ryaner said, 'nobody ever got away from here.'

'How do you know?' said Keaner. ''Cause you're wrong, because somebody did.'

'How?' I asked.

'Two fellas came down to the school. They were dressed like gypsies. They put a spell on the Brothers and then they grabbed a lad, put girl's clothes on him and away they went over the mountains and gone. That's what I heard here years ago.'

'The gypos robbed him, you mean,' I said, 'snatched him?'

'Nobody knows but he never came back anyway.' said Keaner.

The Brothers clapped for silence and as the line moved off towards the school, some of the lads opened up with their towels on the midget flies, leaving thousands of them maimed, scores dead. I took my towel from under my arm and joined in on the attack.

All the hay and dust and sweaty smell was washed away by the sea to some far-off shore, and in its place was a salty taste. We were clean, fresh and new. We marched on past the heather and the blossoms yellow and blue. We came into the village, took a sharp turn to our right and into the school building.

TEN

Mrs Kathleen O'Neill
2 Connolly House
off York Street
Dublin 2

Dear James,

I hope you are well and that you're not in any trouble. I wrote to the Minister for Justice asking him to let you out for the summer holidays but he never wrote back yet. Did you get the five pounds that I sent you down? Everybody at home was asking for you. They love and miss you. Your Aunt is always crying about you. Your Father was asking about you as well. Son, when you get out stay out of trouble 'cause I wouldn't be able to bear it anymore. Eamon Doyle has got himself a job in Linsey's weighing the coal. His mother told me that he hands her a wage every week. None of mine are like that.

May and Kevin Coleman haven't got a place off the Corporation yet. I pray to God they get one, soon. She does nothing and he won't get out of the bed in the morning, although she did say that she would get Anthony a pair of new shoes for his confirmation next week. I can't get down to see you because it's too far for me to travel so I am sending Sue down to Galway on Saturday. I've written to the Head Brother so it will be OK. He'll take you to Galway. I'm also putting three pounds in the envelope. Write if you want more. We all miss you and send our love. Stay out of trouble.

      I love you
      from Mam

P.S. Your Aunt is getting a Mass said for you.

I couldn't wait to see Sue, even the seconds seemed to drag along. I sat in the old Brother's office. Everything the same as the day I got here. I remembered the oul' snail stroking my smokes, the oul' bollix is probably still on the first one. Sitting there, my shoes all shiny and new, my Sunday suit. The Brothers gave me a new vest and underpants but I'd have swapped it all for a pair of long trousers. Beep. Beep. I didn't even hear the car pull up, I was thinking that my sister Sue wouldn't know who I was in short trousers. Beep. Beep. The engine revved up.

'Come along, James.' Brother McCann sat at the steering wheel, white collar, white shirt, fag in his mouth and dark sunglasses. I opened the door on the passenger side, sat in and slammed the door behind me. We were off. On the same road with the same Brother in the same car that had brought me to Letterfrack. Even the people that we waved at on the road looked the same.

'Well, isn't this the life,' Brother McCann said cheerfully, 'your sister coming all the way down here to see you. You're the luckiest boy in the school. Isn't that so?'

'I suppose.'

'You suppose, is that all you can say? And what about me driving you all the way to town, do you think that I have nothing else to do? You're very ungrateful. What about the other boys at the school that have no mammies or daddies, the orphans, would you like to be one of them?'

I didn't answer.

'Would you like me to turn round and go back to the school?'

'No,' I said quickly.

'God but you're a very gloomy lad, what's up? What is the matter with you?'

'Nothing. I'm happy is all.'

'Now you are not to talk about school, is that understood? Not one word about the school. No stories or lies. You are not to talk about what happens here. Is that clear?'

'Yes, Brother,' I replied, thinking about the clatter in the face he gave me the day I ran away and all the other horrible things that had happened.

The Brother lit a cigarette. The windows in the car were closed tightly and so all I had to do was breathe the smoke up my nose quietly all the way to Galway. The train station was jammed with people. I stood with the Brother near the ticket office. He had his dark coat on and looked more like a priest.

'Well, can you see your sister?' he said.

'Na, not yet,' I replied. Maybe she missed the train, I thought, my heart sinking low.

'Come along, let's see if she's outside the station.'

Brother McCann took me by the hand and led me out through the door. Outside, Sue stood with her back to us looking towards the entrance to the station where the cars come in. I smiled, my heart now racing. The Brother let go of my hand just as she was turning in our direction. For a moment I could see an unsure expression move slowly across her face, her eyes searching for something familiar so she could be sure.

'Sue.' It seemed to come out unknown to me.

I watched her face change into a look of amazement as she came towards us.

'Are you James's sister?' Brother McCann broke in, holding out his hand and smiling.

'Yes, that's right. Are you the Brother from the school?'

'I'm Brother McCann. May I speak to you privately for a moment?'

'Sure,' Sue replied. 'Stay there James. I'll be back in a minute.'

They walked a couple of feet away from me and started talking.

I stood, happy to watch the cars and people come and go, hearing the sound from the trains pulling in and pulling out of the station to the echo of a whistle, then the sound of Sue's voice called to me, 'Come on, James.'

I walked over to where they stood. Sue put her arm around my neck.

'OK Brother, I'll have him back here by five o'clock.'

'Good,' said Brother McCann. 'Off you go now, James, and enjoy yourself.'

Sue held me gently and warmly by the neck until we reached Eyre Square. We stopped.

'Jaysus,' she said, 'you're as big as a house and have rosy cheeks like a culchie. You look great. Do you like it down here?'

I could feel myself coming apart and nothing that I did could stop the volcanic eruption. Out it came, tears spurting all over my face, my hands like window-wipers brushing them away.

'Don't cry James … Please, you'll have me as bad as yourself in a minute if you don't give over,' said Sue softly, tears running down from her eyes. Neither of us said a word as I cried and cried. Then it stopped. I must have run out of water.

'Are you alright now?'

'Yeah, Sue,' I said, sniffing, my face damp from all the crying.

'Would you be able to get me a pair of short trousers like them for your da?' she said.

I thought of me da going to work in short trousers and we laughed. We went everywhere, shops, caffs, pubs, street after street. I couldn't believe my eyes when I saw Woolworth's, it was the exact same as the one in Grafton Street. The sun was boiling hot. I was jaded from walking and the water that had stopped coming out of my eyes was now pouring down my forehead. Sue brought me in and out of shops all day, getting me things.

'Are you sure you don't want anything else?'

'No,' I said, barely able to carry the bags that I had.

'Ah well, I'll get something for the kids at home then. Here, hold these.' She handed me her two bags and went along the racks of clothes, picking up jumpers, coats, shirts, more or less anything within hand's reach, and in front of my eyes took a carrier bag from under her coat and dumped all the clothes into it saying, 'Come on, I think that's the lot,' and we marched out of the shop.

'Are we alright?' she said outside on the street.

'Yeah,' I said. Now that I thought about it I hadn't seen her buy anything all day. I looked up again.

'What's wrong with you?' she said.

'Nothing,' I said.

'Let's go so. I'll buy you a nice meal before you go back.'

We walked towards Eyre Square with half of Galway city in the bags. 'In here,' she said pointing towards the door of a flash hotel.

Men with dicky bows stood just inside the glass door. One came over and brought us to a table.

'What do you want, James?' Sue asked in a kind of posh voice.

'Chips and eggs and a bottle of rasberry,' I said.

The man nodded his head and wrote it down on his notebook.

'And I,' said Sue, 'will have the roast pork. And could you bring me a scotch while I'm waiting?'

Sue lit herself a cigarette. She caught me looking at it.

'Here, do you want one?' said she, handing me the lighted cigarette.

I held it in my hand for a minute wondering whether I should go into the jax and smoke it.

'Smoke the bleedin' thing,' said she losing her posh voice for a second. 'Don't mind anybody.'

I puffed away on the long Rothmans. The food came. The man saw me smoking, but he didn't say anything. We ate, drank, smoked and talked about home and the family. Then we took the price and name tags off the gear that was in the bags.

'Here,' Sue said, when we had finished removing the tags, 'don't tell me ma that I brought you out shoplifting down here.'

'What do you think I am?' I said back to her, feeling as if I was being treated like a child again.

The dishes were cleared away and we had tea and another smoke.

'What's that fella like?' said Sue, smoke rushing out of her nostrils and mouth.

'What fella?' I said, looking around the room. 'The Brother that I met with you at the train station. Yer man out of the school.'

'A bastard,' I said, my mind filling with pictures, sounds and smells from the place. 'I don't want to go back. They do things to you. It's awful.'

'You have to,' said Sue, 'sure, you'll be home soon. That Brother told me at the station that you would be coming home for the summer holidays. I'm telling you, if you run away now, you'll get nicked again, put back away, and you'll get no holidays. I swear on me Charley's life he said he'd let you out. Believe me?'

'OK,' I said, believing her, my heart raised a little.

The bill was placed on the table.

'Will that be all?'

Sue nodded, lifted the bill from the table and put on her coat.

'Come on, we have to be at the station soon to meet the Brother. Grab some of them bags.'

She paid for the food. I watched her! We lit another Rothmans each and headed back towards the train station. I saw the Brother as we entered the station. 'Will I run?' I thought to myself. I slowed my walking pace down, hoping that when we got near the Brother Sue would change her mind and say, 'Run for the train.' But it was not her that said it. It was the Brother.

'Quick, quick, you'll miss your train,' he shouted at her.

'Ah Jaysus, hurry James,' said Sue, picking up a faster pace. 'Here, give me the bags.'

I ran alongside, passing her the bags till we got to the platform gate. 'Here,' she said to me, 'open my bag and take the money out.'

128

I did. It was a roll of notes.

'Take what you want.' I took a few fivers. 'That's for yourself,' she said. I put the rest of the money into her bag. 'Well, I'll see you soon. Be a good boy and don't get yourself into any trouble. Go on now. The Brother is waiting for you.'

I could see that she wanted to give me a hug but because of all the bags she couldn't.

'I'll see you then. Thanks for coming to see me and tell them all at home that I'll see them on my summer holidays.'

'See ya,' she said, running down the platform amid the sounds of engine noises, whistles, voices and running footsteps, and ten bags dangling from her arms and hands. She jumped onto the train out of my sight. The footsteps and the voices subsided. The whistle sounded a last loud blast and, before its echo was gone, the last of the carriages wriggled like a snake out of the station and away to Dublin.

When I got back to the school everyone was out in the yard. Brother McCann had already searched my pockets in the small office where the clock ticked near to seven. Ten pounds he counted out. Now I sat with a gang around me asking all sorts of questions. 'Hey Madzer, why didn't you do a moonlight back to Dublin?' 'Did you drink any booze?' 'Any smokes?' Ryaner sat down beside me.

'Fuck bleedin' off, yez dirt birds, he hasn't got anythin',' he said.

Knowing what Ryaner was like, they fucked off.

'You're mad coming back here. If it had a been me, I'd be gone like a swan.' He stopped for a moment. 'Listen,' he started off again, 'did you bring any dough back? Have you anythin' hid?'

I didn't answer him. Instead I looked over at Keaner who was sitting with Ballyer and Fltzy playing cards, but they didn't look all that interested in the game for their eyes were glued to me. I held my eyes on Keaner who was mouthing at me. The message read, 'Have you got anything?' I nodded.

Keaner came over to where me and Ryaner were sitting.

'Come on,' said Keaner, 'let's go on a walk in case the Brother cops on.'

We hadn't done two laps around the yard when Ballyer, Fitzy and Ryaner joined the walk. Ballyer was the first to open his mouth.

'Hey, Neiller, how much did ye bring back for us?'

'Ballyer, I'd give you a boot into your mouth, only I'd be afeared I'd lose me foot, so shut bleeding up,' said Keaner.

'Where have you got the money?' Keaner asked, holding his hands over his mouth so as no one could make out what he was saying, 'cause all you had to do was fart and the rats and squealers would be off to one of the Brothers with a full report. So in case anyone would hear what I was saying other than those that I wanted to hear, I sang out the hiding place.

'Itits ininn myyyy trunksunksunks.'

'In your trunks?' said Keaner in a hushed tone. I nodded.

'Jaysus,' said Fitzy, 'there's probably shit marks all over it.'

We walked around laughing at what Fitzy said. Keaner told Ballyer to shut up 'cause he was laughing too loud and too long. We walked around the yard and all agreed that Ryaner should use the money to buy smokes when he went out to the tech in Clifden and I told Keaner that I'd meet him and Ryaner in the dormo jax after lights out. Then we split up and walked around the yard in different directions until Brother Byrne clapped hands to fall in. I stood in my line in my Sunday suit, feeling happy, feeling a little chill float past my knees where the tops of my socks ended and the legs of my trousers began.

'God,' I thought to myself as I snuggled down deeper into the bed and waited for the lights to go out, they better give me my summer holidays now.

Brother Michael clapped his hands for lights out. I lay in my bed listening to his footsteps as he walked about the dormitory checking that every boy was present. Then he walked back to his own room at the back of the dormo to switch the radio off. The only sound left was the sound of constant breathing broken only by somebody twisting and turning in their bed, the air heavy with hot breath mingled with the warmth of the night.

The beam from the watchman's lamp cut through the darkened corridors like a laser. I watched it move from side to side as he walked towards our dormo almost like a blind man with a stick except the lamp made no sound. He'll be waking the slashers up now to get them to go to the jax in case they piss in the bed. The lamp searched around the dormo slowly moving from bed to bed, tracking down the knotted sheets that lay tied at the end of the sailors' beds. One by one the watchman woke them, six, maybe seven, then marched them off to the loo. The light from the flash lamp cast big shadows out in the corridor. They seemed to move sleepily on the wall, the sound of piss bashing down into the lavatory killing the quietness stone dead. It seemed to last for ages, one after the other straight into the bowl.

They were finished. Quietness had crept back in. The slasher brigade had accomplished their mission and were herded back to bed. The watchman left our dormo to go to St Joseph's where he had his desk. I waited and waited, listening for the sounds that would tell me that he was finished his rounds. The noise from the chair being scraped along the floor and placed beside the table.

The smell of piss in the jax was brutal. It was here that I waited for Keaner and Ryaner, behind the cubicle door, the fiver clenched tightly in my hand, doing my best not to breathe in too deeply while marching on the spot to keep my feet warm against the cold tiled floor. It was tiring so I stood up on the bowl which had a wooden seat.

I heard footsteps come into the jax. I bent over towards the door and slid back the bolt as gently as I could. It made a scraping noise like a cat sliding down a rusty aluminium roof. In a second Ryaner was in the cubicle with me, his back firmly against the door, his finger to his mouth, meaning 'Don't say a word.' I was frightened, sensing danger and knowing that if we were caught by anyone, there would be no end to what would happen to us.

The five-pound note was drowning in my hand from my sweat.

'Where's Keaner?' I asked.

'Give me the fiver,' said Ryaner.

I handed him the money and watched him fold the note into a tiny square. He put it in his pyjamas sleeve and rolled it up his arm.

I indicated to Ryaner that I wanted to go but he didn't move. His eyes, his face had changed. He was older than me, twelve, maybe even thirteen and longer here than I was. I thought about the time we were swimming, he only left me alone when Keaner and Ballyer came and when I got out of the water to dry myself, I sensed him watching me.

Ryaner shoved his hand down the front of my pyjamas. I tried to push him away, to get out the door of the cubicle, but his hand squeezed me tightly round me privates and I could do nothing. It was really sore.

'You did it with Behan didn't you?' he said. 'You like this, don't you?' he whispered. 'Turn around. I want to put it between your legs.'

His voice changed and his hands locked around my waist and he tried to turn me around. I was really frightened. The smell of piss drifted up through my nose, the cold from the stone floor seemed to creep up my spine. He pushed himself against me, harder and harder.

'I'm going to do it to you, I won't be a minute.' His hands were hurting me.

'What's he trying to do?' I thought. The feeling of dirtiness hung like a mist around me.

'Let me go, Ryaner,' I cried.

'Won't be long now,' he said.

'No, no, I have to go.'

He tried to kiss me, his body moving faster, pushing harder against me. 'Hold on just for a minute,' I said, hoping he would loosen his grip.

'OK,' he said.

I moved away from him quickly.

'What's wrong?' he asked.

'I want to go back to my dormo,' I said.

'OK then, if that's the way but before you go, I want a gobble.'

'Come on,' he said, his hand pulling his privates up and down. 'Come on, gobble me or I'll punch the fuckin' head off ya.'

'I'm going to call the Brother, let me go, Brother, Brother!' I called. 'I'll call the watchman.'

'Call the Brother then. Call the watchman. They'll just want to do it to you as well. That's how I found out about it,' said Ryaner, laughing at me.

I slid back the bolt and I was gone. I thought of things me

ma had said to me when I was younger. Feeling dirty, I slid down into my bed. 'What a fool,' I thought, 'What an idiot. I could have been home today.'

I could see the watchman's light heading towards the dormo jax and I wrapped the blankets around me tighter than ever.

ELEVEN

The summer holidays were drawing near and any time I thought of them, I tingled with excitement. So did most of the boys. As I walked around the yard, I was wondering just how many more steps I'd have to walk before I got home. My mind was thinking in millions when Brother McCann's car came into view just outside the workshops. I watched as he opened the back door. Two new boys of about ten or eleven got out and, with Brother McCann holding them by the hand, they were walked down into the yard. For a moment, I thought I knew one of the boys, but then I wasn't sure. The football game stopped and the ball now rolled across the yard with no more force behind it than the breeze. I saw the shock on the two boys' faces as they looked at the short trousers and tight haircuts of us boys. Brother McCann stood waiting for Brother Byrne. They began talking. The two new boys stood awkwardly beside the Brothers. Nobody was interested in the ball that was rolling near the feet of the two Brothers. Then McCann noticed it. With one movement of his foot he whipped up the ball and sent it across the yard. There was a rush for it, because the Head Brother's eyes were watching and it gave the boy who got the ball a chance to show off. Brother McCann pushed the two new boys forward into the game of Gaelic football. They looked lost.

The forms that had been sent for our mothers to sign to get us out on holidays slowly began to arrive back at the school. Mine came too. I couldn't believe it. I had to read the letter dozens of times, and then to make sure, I got some of the boys to read it to me as well. There were boys who would not be going on holidays, but they kept that to themselves, right up until that morning when we marched, carrying our brown cases with our stuff, onto the waiting buses. While the buses filled, I looked up at the faces of the boys that were staying behind, looking out of the windows of the dormo. As the bus moved off, I waved up at Ryaner and Keaner. They didn't wave back.

The bus left the main gate of the school and we all cheered at the top of our voices. We were off, speeding towards Galway, three busloads of boys and Brothers. Each boy was dressed in his Sunday suit and white shirt, short pants, black shoes and grey knee-length socks. Brother Michael and Brother Byrne were on our bus, watching us, telling us to get down off the seats, to stay quiet and to behave ourselves, but the excitement of going home was too much for us. Soon we were humming songs and a while later we sang at the top of our voices, 'We are off to Dublin in the green, in the green ...' We sang all the way and when we stopped singing, the bus in front or the one behind started. The Brothers were chuffed with themselves, because every time we passed someone on the road, or a village or town, people would stare at us and smile and wave and shout, 'God bless you.'

I rested my head against the seat. Going home, going home. My hands got sweaty at the thoughts of it, and my stomach rumbled with nerves and excitement. I could see myself running into the flats, running up the stairs. The hall door would be open and I'd go in and say, 'How are yez?' Then I'd see all my friends, the Doyles, Mucker, Bracken. I wondered what they'd say when they saw me? I held my breath for a moment and squeezed myself with my arms around my shoulders. My mouth watered in my mind's eye I could see chips, eggs, beans, Coca-Cola, crisps … mmmmm, I could almost taste them as the bus reached Galway city.

We drove through Galway city. The Brothers clapped their hands and told us to get our coats back on and comb our hair. This we did at double speed. I could make out the train station as the bus drove down the street.

'Hey, we're here,' I shouted, 'that's the station!'

I shouldn't have opened my mouth. They were all on top of me looking out of my window to see the station.

'Jaysus, doesn't look like a train station to me,' someone said loudly.

Then a stony silence fell on the whole bus as Brother Michael shouted.

'If you don't know how to behave like anything other than animals, this bus will be turned back the way it came, is that understood? Now get back to your seats.'

'Yes Brother,' we all said as the bus came to a halt outside the train station. We sat in our seats, waiting to be called. All the boys who had to get buses home were called first, and the boys who were going to Dublin and all the places that the train stopped at on the way were called last. And it was now our turn. We marched off the bus straight into the station and onto the train. We were placed on seats by the Brothers. I was placed beside Splinter Spillane and Chesty Moore. We sat waiting for the train to move out. Chesty Moore sat eating the fingernails off himself.

Then the carriage was filled with the roar of the engine. The train edged its way out of the station. I could feel the strength of the train as it belted along the tracks towards Dublin. I watched the boys in their seats move gently from side to side as the train slightly moved its hips and slid around a bend. People were now moving from one carriage to another, holding onto anything that would steady them. As the door to the next carriage slid open, a strong breeze would brush past me and my hair would blow up off my head like that of a wild Indian, galloping on horseback after the iron horse. The door closed tight, slicing the breeze in two. My eyes quickly darted towards the window, and at the same time I took cover. The train was being chased by Sioux Indians. My foot reached under the table to Splinter and Chesty, and I tapped them both with my foot. 'What?' said Splinter.

'Indians,' I whispered, so as not to frighten the other passengers, still keeping very low in my seat and pointing out the window. Within seconds Chesty had his Winchester in his hand. I watched him pull back the firing-pin with his thumb, then wet the top of his thumb on his lips and tip the top of his rifle with it, just where the sight is, for luck. When Splinter had finished loading his two six-guns, we all took one look at each other, then I sent the first stick of dynamite sailing out through the shattered glass of our carriage window. Boom, the first of the Indians bit the dust, followed by my two partners opening up with round after round of lead. Arrows zoomed past our heads. Splinter cracked one of the braves that had clung onto the side of the window, swinging his tomahawk right into the mush with the butt of his gun. The fight began to get louder and became more real.

'Aggaag, I've been hit!' screamed Chesty, clutching his stomach.

By now, the boys that sat behind us were peering over at us. 'What's bleeding wrong with yez?'

'Injuns, yez eejits,' said Splinter, sending a couple of rounds out through the window with his imaginary six-shooter. Within seconds, we were being backed up by the Marines, who were stationed on the seat behind us. 'OK men, let them have it!' said whoever was in command back there, in a kind of Dublin-American accent. Tarrar, tarrrrr, went the tommy-guns, zip, then a soft whistle, then bang went the mortar fire. Screams and cheers and groans of agony, then the seat across from the one behind joined in. Some of the boys stretched out their arms and became aeroplanes. They came in fast and low, but it was not the Indians they were after. Before I could let out a warning, the Luftwaffe had dropped tons of bombs on the Marines. Luckily enough, nobody was killed, and the Marines fought back with arrows at their backs and German kamikaze pilots at their front.

Chesty Moore was now engaged in lobbing hand grenades over at the Jerries, and Splinter was hanging over the seat in front of us, radioing for help. The word was no sooner out of his mouth when artillery, disguised as a black shoe, came ripping through the air. It was a direct hit on one of the aeroplanes. 'This is war,' I thought to myself, diving for cover to avoid the volleys of greeners, golliers and heavy-duty phlegm spits that were now filling the skies above my head.

Soon it was every boy for himself. I held my brown case up to my face as a shield from the dirty big spits that were flying in my direction. From where I was under the table I could see a shoeless foot hobbling along the aisle, whoever it was getting riddled with spits. I saw him get his shoe and bash it across some boy's head, then another boy's. Everybody got up from under the tables to see what the commotion was about and who it was. The bloke whose shoe had been thrown around the train was Brother Michael. He stood raging, his clothes crowded with spits. I could see the rage building on his face, and before we had time to get out of his way, he exploded, lashing out clatters and kicks in every direction. He pulled me by the hair and pushed me back into my seat. I didn't see who said it, but all of us heard it, somebody called the Brother a 'poxy bastard'. Instant silence and fear fell over everybody. The train seemed to go quieter. We waited. Brother Michael reached for the nearest boy. He grabbed Chesty Moore between the legs and Chesty screamed in pain. There was a sharp crack as Brother Michael smashed his fist into Chesty's face. The blood shot out of his nose. I could feel my face going white, and I watched as the floor of the train went red. Other Brothers came up to where Chesty was. They looked a bit frightened by all the blood. Brother Byrne spoke to Brother Michael quietly, and Brother Michael went back to his seat. Brother Byrne stood over Chesty.

'Come on now sonny. It's not that bad,' he said mopping the blood off Chesty's face with a spotless white hankie. 'What would your mother say if she knew that you'd been fighting? Come along now boy, it's home on holidays you're going.'

Eventually he got Chesty to stop crying. The blood didn't stop though and his white shirt was drenched. Brother Byrne saw us watching and listening to everything.

'You boys,' he said to us, 'clean up all this mess.'

With that, he took Chesty down through the train. Nobody said a word. Not one sound was uttered for the rest of the journey. Chesty was brought back and put sitting across from the Brothers.

Soon things became familiar to me. Houses, rows and rows of them, that I'd seen the time I got brought on the train by

Kennedy to Galway. I was back in Dublin. I could smell it, see it, taste it.

The train conductor walked through the carriage winking and smiling at us as he passed, calling out 'Next stop Dublin city. This train will terminate at the next stop. Dublin city next stop.' When he saw Chesty's broken face he gave the Brothers a dirty look and then walked out of the carriage.

We didn't have to line up in single file to get off the train. The Brothers got off first, and then we all piled off onto the platform. When everyone was off, we began to walk along the platform towards the gate where we could see lots of people waiting. The Brothers walked beside us carrying suitcases, with their black raincoats slung over their arms.

For the first time in ages I felt like crying. I felt sad, not for myself, but for all of us. It was as if I was standing behind the gate that was in front of me, watching myself and all the other boys walk up the platform. I could see Ma now, waving with one hand and wiping her eyes with her scarf with the other. Sue was with her and so was Martina.

The gates were opened. My ma ran towards me, arms outstretched. Now they were wrapped tightly around me and I could hear her cry. Her grip on me loosened, and for the first time in a long time I looked into me ma's face.

'Ah Ma,' said I, embarrassed, 'it's alright, I'm not a baby.'

'OK, OK son, I won't cry, I won't.'

All around me there were people crying, sobbing. I said goodbye to some of the boys. 'See ya, Splinter, see ya, Fitzy, see youse everyone.' While we said goodbye to each other, all the ma's were drying their eyes and saying, 'Well, at least we have them back.' 'That's true, and them's lovely suits they have there.' 'Thank God they're home now.' There were some da's there too. I looked around to see where Chesty was. For a while I thought that he was gone. There he was, sitting on the long bench with a man and a woman. I could hear their voices rise as Chesty pointed towards Brother Michael. Then all the ma's stopped yapping and began to look over to see what all the shouting was about.

'Oh Jaysus, look at that poor child! What happened to him?' said me ma.

'The Brothers hit him on the train,' I said.

Then the Brothers came up to us to say goodbye.

'Have a nice time, James, see you soon.'

'Goodbye Brother,' I said, while me ma smiled and threw the Brother a dirty look.

'Here, hold on there!'

The man that had been sitting beside Chesty was coming towards the Brothers. He got in front of the Brothers. Next thing, his son was beside him, crying and pointing at Brother Michael.

'It was him, Da.'

'Ya rotten poxy bastard,' shouted Chesty's da. 'How could ye do this to a child?'

Chesty's ma hurried over and pulled his da away.

The rest of the Brothers bundled Brother Michael down the platform.

Sue tapped me on the shoulder and handed me a pair of long trousers. I tied me coat around me waist, pulled off me short trousers and pulled the long ones on.

'Come on son,' Ma said, walking towards the exit, 'they're all waiting for us.'

I looked at the short trousers lying on the platform and kicked them high into the air. They landed on the roof of the train. Splinter Spillane and a few other boys standing nearby saw me and burst out laughing. I put me hands into the pockets of me long trousers. I could hear Chesty's da still cursing and swearing at the Brothers. I stood for a while listening, then I ran out of the train station after me family. Someone called my name. I didn't stop and I didn't look back.